"You won't be able to put thi[s] read totally sucked me in."

MIRANDA KENNEALLY, bestselling author of *Catching Jordan*

"Honest, fun, and entirely compelling, this is a story about how being in the wrong place at the wrong time can lead to a whole lot of right. Tatum is a character you'll relate to, cheer for, and want to befriend."

LAURIE ELIZABETH FLYNN, author of *Firsts*

"An unfailingly entertaining and thoroughly engaging read from cover to cover ... highly recommended."

—MIDWEST BOOK REVIEW

"Christina June's contemporary retelling of Cinderella is a delightful debut that addresses family, friendship, trust, and going for what you really want. A lovely story that's full of heart."

—LAUREN GIBALDI, author of *The Night We Said Yes*

"Tatum's complex and realistic relationships with her friends, family, and a potential love interest will have you savoring every chapter while heavily anticipating the next. *It Started with Goodbye* is an adorable and clever contemporary that will enthrall you with its fairy tale-esque charm."

AMI ALLEN-VATH, author of *Liars and Losers Like Us*

"[A] fun, contemporary take on the Cinderella tale that explores what it takes to be yourself while finding your place in life, love, and your family. June's characters are vividly drawn, complex people that you'll want to root for, and Tatum's story will strike a chord for anyone who's felt like they were misunderstood."

"A sweet and satisfying portrait of family, friendship, and discovering your own path. Tatum's journey from fear and disappointment to honesty and freedom to be herself is one that will resonate with many readers."

"With an adorably charming heroine and a swoon-worthy love interest, Christina June has created true YA perfection."

"A heartfelt and refreshing take on a classic fairy tale, with a modern Cinderella you will root for. Tatum is a complex and realistically drawn protagonist, and the slow-burn romance with her Prince Charming had me grinning and yearning for more."

It Started with GOODBYE

Christina June

BLINK

BLINK

It Started with Goodbye
Copyright © 2017 by Christina June

This title is also available as a Blink ebook.

Requests for information should be addressed to:
Blink, *3900 Sparks Drive SE, Grand Rapids, Michigan 49546*

ISBN 978-0-310-75866-2

Cover design: Darren Welch
Interior design: Denise Froehlich

Printed in the United States of America

17 18 19 20 21 22 23 24 25 /DCI/ 20 19 18 17 16 15 14 13 12 11 10 9 8 7 6 5 4 3

Dedication

"*A strong spirit transcends rules.*"
—Prince Rogers Nelson

*For anyone who has ever had to defend
the things that make them happy.*

Chapter 1

*T*atum, they have your license plate on camera. This is as good as it's going to get." Mr. Alves stood at the head of the table in the plush conference room.

I stared blankly at him, still trying to process what he was saying. My head was spinning, and it sounded like he was speaking Greek while his cheeks were stuffed full of mashed potatoes.

My stepmother, Belén, poked my shin with the toe of her pointy pump. "Tatum Elsea, Mr. Alves is trying to help you."

I yelped, even though it didn't hurt. "You didn't need to kick me," I said loudly, making sure my dad, Mr. Alves, and the people in the next office over heard me.

"Tatum," my dad warned, putting a hand on my shoulder. "Tom, could you please run through the deal again? Tatum, you need to listen. This is your future."

"Yes, sir," I said, eyes down, guilted. The temperature in the room seemed to increase with each second that ticked by on the wall clock. I wiped my palms on my skirt.

Mr. Alves cleared his throat. "Right. Here we go again." He looked at me over his glasses. "You're expected to confirm the figures seen on the security camera at four thirty-seven p.m. on June ninth, exiting Mason's Department Store." He pushed his glasses back up on his nose and glanced down at the paper in his hand. "Ashlyn Zanotti and Chase Massey. Is that correct?"

"Correct," I said, and checked out my reflection in the table's polished surface. This was torture.

"The official charge for both is grand larceny, because the total amount stolen exceeds two hundred dollars. Normally in Virginia, you would be charged with the same felony, since you were the driver. However, as you have no record, you're issuing this statement, and there was no merchandise found on your person or in your car, the commonwealth attorney has agreed to reduce it to a misdemeanor instead."

"Thank goodness for small favors," Belén said. "This is still going to affect your college applications, you know. I was reading on the Focused Parent blog about the impact of criminal charges. You'll have to disclose it, Tatum."

It was so typical of her to bring up that ridiculous blog. Just because the author was an "expert" and was on TV all the time did not make him the authority on life. If I'd had the power to take away her voice temporarily, like in *The Little Mermaid*, I might have used it. I bit the inside of my cheek instead.

"The silver lining is that we can petition to have your record expunged." Mr. Alves offered me a sad smile, while Belén exhaled the biggest sigh of relief the world has ever heard.

"That's good," I said quietly, to the table. At least this snafu wouldn't follow me forever.

Mr. Alves continued. "Mr. Massey, age nineteen, will obviously be charged as an adult."

Had I heard that right? I picked my head up. "Um, Mr. Alves, did you say nineteen?"

"Yes," he said, his glasses sliding lower on his nose. "Why?"

My eyes grew wide. "He told her he was seventeen."

Belén's hair rustled against her blouse as she shook her head, no doubt with disappointment over the ineptitude of teenagers, especially that of my best friend, Ashlyn.

"It seems that Mr. Massey did more than falsify his age. He also chose not to disclose his long list of previous offenses." Mr. Alves flipped through the pages in his hand. "Vandalism, assault, petty theft—it goes on and on."

"Huh." I'd always known Chase wasn't good boyfriend material, for sure not good enough for Ashlyn, and his finer points were sadly the reason I found myself in what the commonwealth attorney wanted to call "the getaway car" that fun-filled afternoon. But a repeat offender? For Ashlyn's sake, I'd tried my best to look past the scruff on his face, the ink peeking from beneath his sleeves, and the way he leered at me when Ashlyn's back was turned. And for my trouble, for trying to watch out for her, it landed me here, in this uncomfortable wooden seat, between my dad and the stepmonster, facing completely ridiculous, unnecessary charges.

"These are the people she's keeping company with?" Belén sat up straighter and eyed my dad from over my head. Not only was she pretty, if you liked robotic, she was tall and often used that to her advantage when she wanted to remind all of us that she was in charge.

"I didn't know, all right?" I protested. "I hope you realize I wouldn't have been spending time with a criminal if I'd been aware of that piece of information."

My dad and Belén exchanged another look I interpreted as skepticism. I was sure that any trust I had earned over sixteen years of being Dad's daughter and eight years as Belén's stepdaughter went right out the window the second the security guard came charging out of Mason's after Chase and Ashlyn, but still, I thought they knew me better. Clearly, I thought wrong.

Dad patted me on the shoulder to remind me that this wasn't the time to argue. I sighed as Mr. Alves called for his secretary to come in and take down my statement. A young redhead sat down next to Mr. Alves with a laptop, and started typing as soon as I began speaking.

"Well, after school that day, Ashlyn had told me she wanted to go to Mason's to get a new pair of flip-flops and some nail polish." The weather was finally warm enough to wear sandals and short skirts, and Ashlyn wouldn't be caught dead with bare toes. "She let me know on our way to the parking lot that Chase was coming, which ticked me off."

"Be polite, Tatum." Belén narrowed her eyes in disapproval.

I sighed and rested my chin in my hand. "I drove because I knew that if I was the one with the wheels, I could make sure we weren't there all day. The less time I spent with Chase, the better." When Ashlyn and I got to my car—the sensible navy hybrid I shared with my stepsister, Tilly, on weekends—Chase's hulking frame was leaning against my trunk. A cigarette dangled between two fingers, smoke curling upward. I wrinkled my nose, not just at the nasty smell but at Chase himself.

"So is it accurate that you questioned Mr. Massey's character right from the beginning of his relationship with Miss Zanotti?" Mr. Alves gestured to the redhead to make sure she got that.

"Of course I did. I know appearances aren't everything, but I never thought he was a good guy." Chase and Ashlyn had been "dating" for a couple of months. They'd met at the gas station where he worked. She spilled fuel on her hands while pumping—possibly on purpose, knowing Ashlyn—and was "forced" to go inside the convenience store and ask for the restroom key. He flirted, she batted her eyelashes, and suddenly my closest friend was involved with someone she knew almost nothing about.

Chase had been Ash's first real boyfriend, but the guys she'd crushed on in the past were good students, wore clothes that were hole-free, and used hair product generously. Chase, on the other hand, told her he'd dropped out of high school due to "family issues" but was planning to "get a GED real soon, baby." She fell for it hook, line, and sinker. I'd hoped he was just something she needed to get out of her system. There was no doubt that her father,

Arthur Zanotti, millionaire real-estate developer, would freak out as soon as he learned his precious princess was spending time with someone like Chase. Luckily for her, he hadn't picked up on that tiny detail of Ash's life. Until now, at least.

"Chase wasn't exactly the kind of guy you'd bring home to meet the parents," I told them. I started doodling on the pad of paper in front of me, until Belén closed her hand over mine, halting the pen from moving. I scowled, but stopped drawing and continued.

"Anyway, I drove to Mason's while Ashlyn and Chase sat in the backseat." Him whispering and her giggling, me feeling like a chauffeur. "After we parked, I went to the art supplies and they went to the makeup." I remembered wandering through the racks of crayons and markers, grabbing a set of charcoal pencils and a small sketchpad that would fit perfectly in my favorite hobo-style shoulder bag.

"And then what?" Mr. Alves nodded for me to keep going.

"I went upstairs to check out the tablet computers." I was saving to buy one, but babysitting money only went so far. I almost passed out when I saw the price for the one I'd been admiring, which had led to a disappointed sigh. I still hoped that by the end of the summer, maybe, I would score enough cash to get it.

"Lynn, make sure you make a note about our client having been in the electronics department," Mr. Alves said to his secretary. "Tatum, did you notice anything odd while you were there?"

"On my way back downstairs to pay for my stuff, I saw Ashlyn and Chase making out in the cell phone aisle. That made me want to throw up, so I turned around immediately and went to pay." Ashlyn had been up on tiptoe, her mouth suctioned to Chase's, while his hands roamed over her back. Blech. I liked kissing as much as the next girl, but in the middle of a store, where anyone could walk by? No thanks. I'd sent Ash a quick text telling her I'd be in the car and not to take all day.

"You didn't happen to notice any Mason's employees near them?"

"Nope." I paid for my pencils and pad, went to the car, and pulled it up in the loading zone, hoping they'd see me when they came out.

"Okay, and what happened when they exited?"

"When they finally came out, Chase went to open the backseat door, but it had automatically locked." When he couldn't get in, his face had turned stormy. I had fumbled with the buttons to let them in, which in hindsight was probably lucky. Those extra few seconds were enough time for the Mason's security guard to come marching out, black walkie-talkie in hand, shouting.

"Once the guard showed up, things started getting bad, fast."

The doors had finally unlocked, and Chase clambered into the car, knocking his elbow into the metal doorframe in the process. He swore loudly. I looked behind me at Ashlyn, who was cowering next to him like she wanted to slide down under the seat in front of her. The security guy pounded on Chase's window so loudly, I screamed.

"Shut up, Tatum." Chase had glared at me in the rearview mirror with his teeth bared, like he was ready to bite me. I looked away and found myself eye to eye with the livid security guard, gesturing for me to roll down the window. I did.

"Is something wrong, sir?" I'd clasped my hands in my lap to keep them from shaking.

"You and your friends need to exit the vehicle, miss."

Mr. Alves glanced over his secretary's shoulder to make sure she was getting all of this. "Go on."

"I got out of the car right away. Ashlyn did too." With what can only be described as a guilty look on her face, eyes downward, refusing to look at me or the guard. "Chase foolishly remained seated and cursed at the guard, until three more came and physically removed him from my car." The men had patted us down; legs spread, arms wide like wings. I'd never been so utterly embarrassed in my life. Even though the evening air was warm and humid, I'd shivered on the sidewalk, waiting to find out what was going on.

"They got nothing from me and Ash, obviously, but I guess you know what they found on Chase." The men pulled four brand-new iPhones from Chase's ragged jeans, and a stack of gift cards from the waistband of his boxers.

Mr. Alves checked his papers. "The monetary amount Mr. Massey stole totaled over three thousand dollars, and it seems he had a little help from a Mason's employee, who left the locked cases open for him and activated the cards."

"What a jerk," I said under my breath.

We had taken a little ride in the cop cars that showed

up minutes later, and Ashlyn and I ended up together. I remembered looking at her pointedly as we sped to the station.

"Did you know he was going to take that stuff, Ash?" She didn't answer me. I stared harder, hoping the weight of my glare might force her to turn her head, but no dice. "Ash? Did you know? Did you help him? Because if you did, you not only put yourself in danger, but me too. I thought you were smarter than this." It was a cheap shot, and I knew it.

At *smarter*, she'd turned her head, her blue eyes neon with emotion. "Everything is going to be fine. This isn't a big deal. Why are you being such a brat?"

My cheeks flamed. "Excuse me? Not a big deal? You and your loser boyfriend shoplift and try to use me as your getaway driver, and I'm getting scolded for being mad? No way. This could ruin our lives. You do not get to call me a brat. I have every right to be upset. You do not. Right now, you don't get to be anything." I glanced forward and realized the policeman driving the car was watching us in his mirror.

Ashlyn waved her hand, dismissing me. "Whatever. We didn't do anything wrong. Chase's friend gave him the phones. He said he put them on layaway and they could be paid for in installments. It'll all get sorted out."

I'd gaped at her. Who was this person, and what had she done with my intelligent, fun, loyal best friend? "If you believe that, there's a beach in Antarctica I'd like to sell you."

My cheeks warmed with anger again, just recalling

that awful scene. Next to me, my dad squeezed my hand under the table.

"So just to wrap this up, you talked to someone at the police station, and you were then released to your father, correct?" Mr. Alves leaned back in his chair, appearing satisfied with my answers.

"Yep." When we pulled in, Mr. Zanotti was already there, wearing his ever-present dark suit, perfectly coordinated pressed shirt, and shiny tie, with cell phone in hand, shouting almost as loud as the security guard had. As soon as I stepped out of the cruiser, my dad's sedan parked next to us.

Once we'd answered their questions, the police finally let Ashlyn and me leave. When I slid into the front seat of Dad's car, I spied Ashlyn in her father's black SUV, the car he carted his clients around in, clearly getting an earful from Daddy. Her eyes were pointed at the floor, as they had been for most of the evening, and I thought I saw a tear falling down her pale cheek. For half a second, I felt bad for her . . . and then I remembered how we'd gotten here.

The ride home was just as uncomfortable for me as I'm sure it was for Ash. I gave up trying to defend myself when my dad started using words like "disappointed," "unsafe," and "poor judgment." Hearing how I wasn't living up to my potential stung. When he said it made him sad that I hadn't come to him when I first realized my friend was dating someone I didn't trust, my heart broke a little. I couldn't find the voice to say I thought I could handle the situation by myself.

In the past when I screwed up, my dad had given me

the proverbial eyebrow raise and let Belén deal with my consequences. She had very specific thoughts on right and wrong. And if I felt she'd been too harsh, he'd always found a way to smooth it over quietly—when she wasn't looking, of course. Which meant his speech hurt that much more, because I knew he felt I'd let him down. It felt like we'd crossed some kind of barrier I didn't even know existed.

At the house, Belén stood in the kitchen, hands on her hips, mouth turned down in an angry frown. Tilly was at the kitchen table, AP Calculus book open, punching the buttons on her graphing calculator. She didn't even bother to lift her head when we came through the door.

"Well?" Belén's tone was sharper than her favorite steak knives. Tilly finally looked up at me with feigned interest. Actually, she was probably very interested, but she'd never let on.

"Well nothing," I replied, immediately going into evasive mode, my best defense against the stepmonster. I poked my head into the refrigerator and pulled out a ginger ale.

Dad cleared his throat. "We have a meeting with Tom Alves scheduled. It seems the girls may be charged with grand larceny."

Tilly's eyes got so big, I thought they might fall out of her head.

Belén's finger tapped her hips like she was itching to wave it at me, and her face was a blotchy patchwork of pink and red. I'd never seen her this mad. "*May* be?"

"Well, Tom's going to dig around and see if he can

find anything to use as leverage. We'll discuss it with him after he speaks with the commonwealth attorney."

I opened the soda can with a loud popping noise, and tiny droplets of ginger ale splattered my nose. I wiped them away and backed myself up against the counter, cold marble pressing into my back.

Belén let out an annoyed sigh. "How can you be so casual about this, Tatum? Do you know what you've done? The danger you put yourself in?" She could be a little dramatic sometimes. It was probably all her time spent in litigation. And on the parenting blog.

I took a slow sip of my soda, swallowed, and eyeballed her. "Yes, I know exactly what I've done. And that would be a big fat nothing wrong. The only thing I'm guilty of is trying to protect my friend from her sketchy boyfriend, and failing. No, I didn't know he was going to steal that stuff. No, I didn't help him. My plan was to go to Mason's, buy some pencils, maybe help Ashlyn pick out some nail polish, and come home. Contrary to popular belief, a field trip to visit our city's finest was not on my agenda today. So can everyone please calm down?"

Belén's jaw clenched shut and her eye started twitching. I wondered if steam might start coming out her ears next. Tilly had turned her face back to the math book, but I knew she was listening and probably filing this conversation away for later. My dad remained quiet, a sign of danger. My father is a pretty thoughtful man. He ponders his words before he speaks, and the majority of time he's able to come up with a solution, if needed, and to say it calmly. But when he stayed in his head too long, I knew it was because he didn't know what to say, or was afraid to say what he was thinking. That conveniently made it easier for him to defer to Belén, who was always happy, thrilled even, to speak up.

He finally shook his head and, barely above a whisper, said to me, "Tatum, please go to your room for the rest of the night." I opened my mouth, like a bass about to bite, and then shut it. There was no use arguing against that point. I'd wait until everyone had calmed down and then plead my case again. I climbed the stairs and didn't look back.

"And here you are with me. Thank you for being candid, Tatum." Mr. Alves continued reading me the terms of our agreement with the CA. "You're being asked to pay a fine of five hundred dollars by September first."

"Which you will be paying out of your pocket," Dad said. I groaned. Goodbye tablet.

"The CA is also requiring one hundred hours of community service. You can choose the location as long as there's a supervisor who can sign off on the paperwork. Same completion date as the fine."

Somehow, I knew that was coming. "And Chase and Ashlyn? Am I allowed to know about them?"

"Mr. Massey's fate will be decided at his trial. I feel confident saying he's likely going to jail."

I sucked in a breath. "Ash?" I whispered.

He looked at his papers. "It appears all charges against Miss Zanotti are being dropped. Perhaps she provided some additional information about Mr. Massey."

I was glad Ash wasn't facing jail time like Chase. I was

decidedly not glad that she was getting off scot-free. I kept that precious thought to myself.

My lawyer stood, marking the end of our meeting. "Ken, Belén, always a pleasure. I'm sorry this meeting wasn't under better circumstances, but I think for the most part, this issue ends here."

I was so glad he thought so.

Chapter 2

*I*n terms of life events, my getting arrested was either pretty horrible timing or pretty perfect, depending on who you were talking to. I was thankful it was June, and a week away from the last day of school. I wouldn't have to see my classmates and listen to the rumor mill blow this out of proportion for long. It would be forgotten by the time school started after Labor Day, in favor of who broke up with who and where so-and-so was applying early to college. I could spend my summer not going to the beach, not hanging out with my friends, and not staying out late in quiet solitude. I hoped, anyway.

On the flip side, Dad was leaving. He worked for the State Department and was forever being sent to faraway countries—this time to Botswana for eight weeks—in order to bring magical, democratic diplomacy to people who supposedly needed him more than I did. Dad and I, despite all the changes that had happened in our family during my lifetime, had always been allies. I was used to him being gone, but I wasn't used to him leaving and being mad at me.

As if I wasn't feeling bad enough about my situation, he decided to lay down some new rules for me to follow in his absence. He chose his last dinner at home to share them, having wonderful timing himself.

"Tatum, you know Belén and I are disappointed by your recent actions."

"I know, Dad." I wanted to wave a magic wand and remove this whole mess from everyone's memories. Mine included.

"We have discussed the situation, and while we applaud you for trying to protect Ashlyn, it does not negate the fact that you put yourself in a very dangerous situation, and we are unwilling to let that slide without some consequences. While I'm gone, your stepmother will be in charge." Like she wasn't in charge all the time, anyway? I slipped my hand under the table and into my pocket, running a finger over the warm metal of my keychain for confidence.

"If you are not babysitting, you will be performing your community service or you will be here. If you want to go on any type of outing, or participate in an activity, Belén needs to authorize it first."

I narrowed my eyes and slid them back and forth between my dad and Belén. "So, this is house arrest. She's my jailer, is what you're saying."

Dad sighed. "That's an ugly word, but yes, in a nutshell."

Excellent. If the police weren't going to lock me up, the stepmonster would. "Great," I muttered under my breath.

Belén frowned, the edges of her mouth dipping so low toward her chin, I thought her face might crack. "Your father and I wish you had let a trusted adult know Ashlyn was in trouble with this Chase character, but that didn't happen. And now you need to accept the consequences."

"Well, the state of Virginia has already helped you out in that department. I'd say a five hundred dollar fine is a pretty big consequence for doing nothing. I get that you want me to learn this life lesson, but it's completely unnecessary." I knew I was being rude, but I didn't care. "Though it's not like I have anyone to hang out with, anyway," I mumbled. Ashlyn hadn't said a word to me since we left the police station.

Belén folded her hands, laid them on the table, and squared her shoulders. She was intimidating, for sure, but I wasn't going to cower. I needed to keep my dignity intact, after all, if I was going to be contending with her by myself for two months. Her expression softened a little when I didn't look away, and she sighed before speaking again. "In addition, my mother will be moving in with us for the summer, so when I'm at work or in court, you'll need to listen to what she says."

My eyebrows shot up. Blanche was moving in? I knew this was meant to be another punishment, when really Belén's mother, Tilly's abuela, was secretly one of my favorite people. I mean, I hardly knew her since she'd visited a grand total of two times in the eight years we'd been a happy little family, but it was obvious to anyone with half a brain that she didn't seem to subscribe to Belén's parenting style. And in my book, that made her a rock star.

I nodded. "Sure thing." A chilly, hard stare came back, and I looked away from Belén. I didn't want my forehead to freeze.

"I mean it, Tatum. I'll be working, and as you know, Tilly will be participating in the District Ballet Company's summer intensive." A small, satisfied smile crossed her lips, as per usual whenever Belén was discussing her daughter's accomplishments.

Tilly was a classically trained ballerina, and even my cranky self couldn't deny that she was a really good one. She'd been in a specialized dance program for three years now. When Tilly got her acceptance letter to McIntosh High School for the Arts, Belén and my dad took us all out to a fancy dinner to celebrate. A year later, I got one thanking me for applying to the visual arts program, but sadly there was no spot for me in the freshman class. No dinner that time. Tilly had also spent the last few summers participating in courses led by frou-frou dance companies all over the country. Belén insisted Tilly stay close to home this year so she could work on her college essays: in other words, so Belén could edit them for—I mean *with*—her.

"Sounds like a plan." There was nothing left for me to do but just go with it.

"One more thing, Tatum." Belén held her palm out. "Car key, please."

"Excuse me?" My fingers tightened around the metal in my pocket.

My dad nodded at me, punctuating the request. I slowly pulled the keys out of my pocket and winced while putting them on the table. As Belén reached out, I snatched them away from her. "Hold on a second." I carefully removed only the car key, leaving my house key still attached to the thick silver rectangle of my keychain. I pushed the car key to Belén, eyes stuck on my dad.

The wrinkle in his forehead softened, and the hard line of his mouth tipped into a sad smile. He came over to my chair and offered me a half-hearted side hug. "You know we love you, honey." I did. Love wasn't the issue here. Even though he was speaking those special words— the ones that seal the pact between parent and child, that assured he'd always have my back—somehow it felt like he and Belén were now on one side of that invisible line, and I was on the other.

"I know, Dad."

"I want you to know that I'm trying very hard to put myself in your shoes."

He was? Could've fooled me. He was the parent who would sneak me dessert when Belén decided I didn't deserve it. He was the parent who consoled me when I got a low test score, and paid attention to when my colored pencils had been sharpened down to nubs and replaced them without my asking. Belén was the one who preferred to dole out discipline like Halloween candy.

"And I'd like you to try just as hard to put yourself in my shoes too. Think about what happened from my point of view, Tatum." Okay. I nodded, wondering where he was going with this. "You are the most important person in my life. In my eyes, you have been extremely lucky in this situation." Was he kidding? "Spending time with Chase, even with the best of intentions, was incredibly risky. Something much worse than a fine and a misdemeanor charge could've happened to you. I want very much to trust that you're going to make the right decisions when you're on your own, and this time, there was a better choice. Can you at least see where I'm coming from?"

I opened my mouth to say something smart, but then shut it. I wanted to point out that he wasn't just an observer of this disaster, that he knew me deep down, that I wouldn't willingly put myself in harm's way. But the look on his face was so final, so decisive, that I couldn't. Was it possible this one slip up scared him into not trusting me?

"If you want to be treated like an adult again, you need to show us that you can behave like one. I know you think we're being unreasonable. But I hope that by the end of the summer, we will all be on the same page, ready to start fresh. You'll see. Let's use this time apart to really think, both of us. I will if you will."

I nodded, not really sure of what I was agreeing to, but still too shaken to speak due to the combination of shame and confusion warring with each other in my head.

"I love you, Tatum. More than anything."

"I know. I love you too, Dad."

He left first thing the next morning, and I was alone.

After Dad left, I holed up in my room the whole weekend under the guise of studying for final exams. When I'd had enough of balancing chemical equations and analyzing *Animal Farm*, I took a break from my books and pulled out my laptop. It was boxy and heavy and ran slower than I would like, but it worked. And it was mine, which was really all that mattered. For what seemed like the millionth time, I checked my email. Nothing from Ashlyn. I didn't expect it at this point—it had been a couple days since what my family was referring to as "the incident"—but that didn't stop me from hoping she might apologize.

Right. Wasn't going to happen. I sighed.

Like I always did when I needed something to make me forget life for a minute, I pulled up Photoshop and opened my current project. I was working on a logo for this girl Abby's blog. She wrote for the school paper and was planning to launch a personal website over the summer. She'd asked me to make something up for her that she could stick on her site, her social media accounts, business cards, and "anything else I might need. A girl needs to advertise, you know," she'd said. "How much do you charge?" She'd pulled me aside in our English class a couple weeks ago.

"No, I couldn't charge you." I was surprised she'd even asked. I just played around with graphics for fun.

"Why the heck not? You're good. You could be making some serious bank." Abby and I weren't close—we'd only met this year in school—but I liked her. She told it like it was. We had worked together on a project earlier in the year, and I'd designed the slide show we presented to the class—complete with my own graphics, of course.

"Huh," was my only answer. I hadn't considered getting paid for my work, but maybe she was on to something.

I finished cleaning up the logo, which I was super proud of, and sent it off to Abby the moment I was done. She wrote me back in seconds.

> Unbelievable about Ashlyn Zanotti, right? And with only a few days left in the year too.

My heart stopped.

> What now? What are you talking about?

> I thought you would have known? She left school. Shipped off to some boarding school in the mountains. Valley something or other.

Oh. My. Goodness. I didn't know whether to cry or laugh. Blue Valley Academy. The private, girls-only school with the big price tag and even bigger set of expectations the students had to follow. Whenever Ashlyn stepped out of line, her *father's* line, he threatened to send her there to "shape up." He had brochures posted around the house as reminders to follow his rules—rules which were eerily similar to Belén's, though no one ever offered to send me away.

The strictness of our homes was one of the things Ashlyn and I whined together about, and often. She told me once that I was her favorite person because I let her just be herself. I thought the exact same thing about her. The nights she slept over, giving both of us an escape, were filled with some of my best memories over the last few years. We'd shut my door, turn on the music, and have colossal dance parties, complete with hairbrush microphones and rock star makeup.

It seemed Mr. Zanotti had followed through on his threat, something I don't think Ashlyn ever believed he'd do. Bet she wasn't laughing about it now.

Great logo, btw. Change the color to purple and I'm sold.

I smiled to myself, pleased Abby liked my design.

Thank you. I like the way it came out too.

She responded again in lightning-quick speed.

Of course I'll be giving you credit on my site. Hopefully get you some more clients.:-)

Clients? I'd need to start my own freelance business if this was going to be a real thing. But the idea of getting paid to do something I loved, I had to admit, was kind of electrifying. The gears of my brain started turning as I conjured visions of me becoming a small celebrity at school, followed by a spot at the college of my choice, and eventually leading to a job, maybe as a designer for a publishing house or advertising firm. I drummed my fingers on my chin. This could work out nicely for me if I played my cards right.

But try as I might, business plans never materialized in

my head, because I couldn't stop thinking about Ashlyn. Feeling particularly lonely and riled up, my body itched inside my skin, until I couldn't sit still and concentrate anymore. Ashlyn's perfectly highlighted blonde head flashed before me, with the same teary expression I'd seen on her face when she was sitting in her father's car at the police station. I knew she was mad at me due to her radio silence. If our roles had been switched, I'd be mad at her too, but I'd like to think I'd give her a chance to explain. And since she was hours away at some secluded private school, my only chance for peace, or at least the ability to focus for more than ten seconds, depended on technology.

A quick search for Blue Valley Academy yielded their pristine website, complete with pictures of wholesome teenage girls in plaid skirts carrying hardback books and field hockey sticks. None of them had on eyeliner or showed bare knees, two things every parent knew were the gateways into delinquency. I scanned the menu bar items and found one that said "student directory." With a few clicks, I had Ashlyn's shiny, expensive new email address.

I sucked in a quick breath. My hands hovered over the keyboard, paralyzed. Why was I nervous? She was the one who needed to be apologizing to me. I willed my fingers to move and managed to slowly open my email and type AZanotti@bva.edu into the "to" field. The cursor winked at me, taunting.

Despite being supportive and witty and so many other wonderful things, Ashlyn was a grudge holder. More than once, I'd seen her go at least a month without speaking to her father. Those were the days she'd spend more time at my house than hers. In addition to our trademark dance parties, we would read celebrity gossip magazines, play gin rummy, and practice braiding each other's hair into crowns and fishtails. A good diversion for both of us, really. But she would never give in and talk to him until her mom paved the way for her, smoothing things over with her dad. I knew Ashlyn wasn't suddenly going to change her stripes just because it was me she was angry with.

I told myself that there were two ways I could approach this. I could just go for it, put myself out there and write a huge long confession, explaining what happened that fateful day from my point of view, telling her exactly why I couldn't lie to defend her and Chase, and beg her to move on. But it probably wasn't the time for that. If I unloaded while she was furious, it would guarantee me an empty inbox, probably forever, and our friendship would go from virtually nonexistent to dead on arrival.

I'd have to be subtle. Casual. I wouldn't mention the whole grand larceny business at all. Maybe a few jokes and jabs would get the ball rolling. I started crafting a letter, each key cool and hard under my fingers.

Hi Ashlyn,

Would she get stabby if I was formal, or would she think I was being contrite? I took off the *lyn*.

Hi Ash,

I heard through the grapevine that you enrolled at Blue Valley. I checked out the website, and it pretty much looks too good to be true. Do you ride to class on horseback? I bet they feed you nothing but ambrosia and Perrier too. We miss your face around here.

We or I? I left it *we*.

You aren't missing anything at all at Henderson. Three more finals and then hello, junior year.

Remember the logo I was working on for Abby Gold's blog? I finished it, and it turned out pretty well. Abby thinks I should make this a regular thing and launch my own business. What do you think?

Maybe she'd bite and give me her opinion. I did actually want it—she was pretty savvy when it came to people-oriented things, Chase excepted. I really just hoped she'd write me back.

Anywho, hope things are going okay. Do you have a roommate? If yes, if she annoys you, you can always freeze her bra or something. My intel says that's the kind of prank people pull at all-girls schools.

Tatum

Or should I sign it Tate? Ashlyn was the only person who ever called me that. Again with the formal name or not. I looked back up at the top of the email. I supposed they should match, so I changed it.

Tate

Oh crud. What about a closing? Did I say *Love* or *Sincerely*? *Warmly*? *Yours truly*? The cheeky but effective

Cheers? Or, my least favorite of all because it was so sadly insincere and fake, *Best*? Why was this so difficult? I closed my eyes for a moment, the pores on my hands prickling. I googled "how to close a letter," determined to find exactly the right way to show my friend that I missed her and wanted to talk with her, but that I wasn't going to apologize because I'd done nothing wrong and acted out of self-preservation. Google would know the right answer.

I read the almighty Wikipedia page titled "Valedictions"— apparently, that was the fancy word that meant *how to say goodbye*—and laughed at some of the phrases people used to write in old letters. "Yours aye"—which meant "yours always"—made me think of a pirate. The list of more casual closings suggested *TTFN*. That was too childish. *Yours hopefully*? Plain desperate, and too obvious. Couldn't give it all away. And then I saw it. *Be well*. It made the most sense, as I was innocently hoping she was settling in at her new school. It wasn't reciprocal. With a simple *Be well*, I was offering my personal goodwill without asking for anything in return. And it wasn't too stiff or laid-back. Just right, as Goldilocks would say.

> Be well,
> Tate

Before I could change my swirling mind again, I pressed *send*. I felt a little lighter than I had when I'd started writing, but half a second later the anxiety of waiting for a response overtook me, and my hands began shaking. I slammed the laptop shut, rattling my desk in the process, and flung myself onto the bed.

Chapter 3

The Tuesday after my dad left for the wilds of Botswana, Blanche arrived.

Belén had anxiously fixed up the basement guest room in a way I could only assume she hoped would please her mother, moving the knickknacks from place to place before settling them and beating the wrinkles out of the throw pillows. She'd even put up a gorgeous poncho— all cream, red, and navy—on the wall like a tapestry. I'd never seen her go to so much trouble to make sure something was just right.

When I was checking out her handiwork, I reached out to the poncho, only to admire it. Belén moved my hand away.

"Tatum. Please do not touch that. You'll get something on it." She scowled and walked out of the room.

I held my hands up in front of my face to inspect

them. Not a speck of grease, ink, or any other errant substance to mess up her precious decoration. The woman really needed to pay attention more often. I worked in pixels, not paints.

When Blanche showed up, via a yellow taxi driven from the airport, Belén instructed Tilly and me to stand side by side on the short walk leading up to the front door.

"Stand up straight, girls." Belén smoothed down her black pencil skirt and locked her knees, the heels of her three-inch patent leather pumps cemented together. I hoped she wouldn't fall over. Or maybe I hoped she would. Tilly, dressed almost identically to her mother, squared her shoulders and stuck her chin out. She stood beside me, just close enough to give the impression we were united, but definitely far enough away that we weren't touching.

I think that if Tilly and I were not forced to be family, we might have been friends. And by friends, I mean people who exchange words sometimes, perhaps ask how the other is doing, show concern when something is going downhill. Instead, as stepsisters, we were mostly two ships passing in the night.

Our parents got married one year after meeting on Match.com, and four years after my own mother had left us for the supposed better offer from her boy toy. I've always been told my mom had been a "free spirit" and "her own person," which pretty much means she was selfish and decided being a wife and a parent weren't for her anymore. It made sense that my dad would choose someone who was more family-oriented and responsible the second time around. He and Belén had a civil ceremony attended only by Blanche and my grandparents, who are now deceased.

I was super excited to have a sister. As awesome as Dad was, having someone my own age around to play dolls with and make pillow forts with and watch cartoons with sounded like the best thing ever. The minute Belén and Tilly moved in, I wanted to take back that thought. Belén didn't believe in idle time for children. Or adults, actually. Tilly took piano lessons, ballet lessons, and martial arts classes three afternoons a week. The other days were strictly for schoolwork. Tilly wasn't allowed to watch any TV until she had completed not only her daily homework but also an additional hour of practice in whatever subject Belén chose for that day. And the only TV she was allowed to watch was educational. Animal documentaries all around!

Belén, obviously thinking only of my best interests, tried to use the same system for me. Dad hadn't had time to put me in lessons or sports before, and it sounded like fun, so we both agreed. At my first ballet lesson, I figured out that tulle is itchy and I had two left feet. I also didn't so much like watching myself stumble around in a gigantic mirror. In Tae Kwon Do, I talked back to the instructor one too many times, and they politely offered my dad our tuition money back if he agreed not to bring me again. Piano went slightly better because I picked up on patterns quickly. But I hated to practice with a passion that burned hotter than a thousand suns, which got me into more than a little trouble with Belén.

"You will never succeed unless you practice. Do the work, Tatum," she preached.

My eight-year-old lips quivered. No one had ever spoken to me like that. Not my teachers. Certainly not my daddy. I was scared speechless, and for the first time ever, something that felt like disappointment set in. Belén watched over me like a hawk when it was time to practice, staring so hard, I felt like I might sink through the piano bench and into the carpet. I started making excuses as to why I couldn't play. At first, I was hungry. So she would fix me a snack and point toward the piano. And then I had to go to the bathroom, where I purposely took ten minutes longer than I needed. In a matter of days, Belén caught on to me and shut down my shenanigans. So there I sat, resenting her for making me sit on the ugly bench and play the ugly notes that stopped making sense because I just didn't want to do it. I dug my heels in, or my fingertips as the case was, and didn't play. I let my hands hover over the keys, an inch of air between me and the ivories, and didn't move.

"You're wasting time, Tatum." Belén glared at me.

"I don't want to." I tried to make my glare as forceful as hers, but I'm sure I was just amusing her.

"Tatum, I will give you until the count of five to begin your scales, and if you do not comply, you will go to your room for the rest of the night."

I hesitated. "Fine."

"Fine what?"

"I'll go to my room." I stood up from the bench, took the stairs up to my bedroom, and shut the door. No one came to tell me dinner was on the table, and my stomach rumbled. I got into bed, pulled the covers up to my chin, and read *Charlotte's Web* until the sun had gone down and the sky was completely black. As my eyelids were beginning to droop, my door opened and my dad came in.

"Having a rough night?" He sat down on the bed with me.

Tears pricked the corners of my eyes. "I don't want to play."

He smoothed my hair back and kissed the top of my head. "I know, sweetheart. But don't you want to be successful at something?"

I'd never heard him say "successful" before.

"That's what Belén says," I said, pouting.

He sighed. "She just wants what's best for you, honey." How did she know what was best for me? She'd never asked me what I liked to do or what I wanted to try.

"I don't like it anymore, Daddy," I whispered, wiping away the water threatening to drop down my cheeks.

"Would you do it for me?" He sounded as unsure as I was. Guilt was a new tactic for us.

The waterworks came on in full force, and I buried my face in his chest, unable to speak. My chest heaved up and down so violently, my cheek felt raw from the friction against my dad's shirt. He held me tight until I calmed down a little bit, stroking my hair in silence.

"Will you at least think about it?" he ventured tentatively.

I stuck my face in the crook of his arm and shook it.

He sighed again, more deeply, giving in. "I'll talk to your stepmother."

Eventually, piano disappeared from my social calendar and I found myself in art lessons instead, which quickly became my happy place. But the car rides there, as Belén shuttled me to the community center and Tilly to her dance studio, were silent and uncomfortable. For years.

Standing next to Tilly, waiting for the cab door to open, reminded me of that initial awkwardness between the two of us. Maybe if we'd been able to bond over a shared interest, like dance, we could have forged some kind of friendship, but I accepted long ago that it just wasn't meant to be. I always believed some of that was because of Tilly, and some, maybe most, came from Belén's desire for her child to only have what she deemed to be positive influences. Which didn't include the step-child who wouldn't stick to the approved plan, it seemed. Never mind the fact that I was regularly praised by my instructors and earned good grades in my classes at school.

Tilly and I exchanged exactly zero words while we waited for Blanche, proof that our frosty acquaintanceship remained intact.

The back door of the cab finally cracked, and a tiny foot sporting a leopard-print ballet flat stepped out onto the pavement. The rest of her equally tiny body emerged, all in form-fitting black, and I raised the other eyebrow, impressed with what good shape Blanche was in for a woman in her late sixties. Self-consciously, I glanced down at my own very average-sized, very average-curved body and shrugged.

At last Blanche's head popped up, and I found myself smiling at her before I could stop myself from showing positive emotion. Her face, just as perfectly made as her daughter's, only showed the slightest hint of age. If I passed her on the street, I probably would have guessed mid-fifties, max, when I knew she was at least ten years older than that. Her golden skin was still mostly smooth, only betraying her age around the eyes and the mouth, leaving me wondering if she laughed a lot. I hoped so. Her eyes were kind as she surveyed us and her new domain.

The cab driver stepped out and popped the trunk. Blanche motioned to us, the receiving line, to help with her bags. Belén sighed loudly. Interesting. Tilly stalked forward, spine aligned like someone had shoved a metal rod up there, and I followed quickly, my own posture resembling that of someone who spent hours slumped over a keyboard.

Belén stood in front of her mother and paused, like she was trying to decide if she should kiss her or offer her a hand to shake. Blanche made the decision for her by putting her hands on her daughter's shoulders and kissing both her cheeks. Belén put her arms around her mother stiffly, in perhaps the most awkward embrace ever witnessed. I stifled a giggle, and caught Tilly glaring at me.

"What is your problem?" I whispered out the side of my mouth. She said nothing.

Blanche released Belén and turned to Tilly. "Matilda, darling, how are you?" Though I knew she'd lived in the US for decades, her voice was still delicately accented.

"I'm well, thank you, Abuela."

Blanche rubbed Tilly's arms. "I'm glad to hear that, sweetheart." Then she winked at me, and I instantly smiled.

"And Tatum, let me look at you, dear," she said, holding me at arm's length and raking her deep brown eyes over me. It was oddly unnerving.

I stood stock still, the warmth of her hands on my arms, waiting for her to finish her assessment. She nodded once, let me go, and charged toward the house. The rest of us stood there in the June sunshine until Blanche shouted, "Come on, slowpokes!" I picked up the floral suitcase the cab driver had handed me and took off after her, Tilly and Belén reluctantly following.

Blanche was down the stairs already when I crossed through the front door. When I reached her room, I found her surveying her new digs, clicking her tongue. "I haven't seen this in years." She gestured with her little chin at the poncho. I wasn't sure if she expected me to comment, but I did anyway.

"I think Belén thinks it'll make you comfortable. Remind you of home, maybe?" I'd never been to Blanche's house, but I thought it was perfectly reasonable to assume she might have some traditional Chilean pieces for her own home.

Blanche clicked her tongue again. "I'm sure she does." What did that mean? There was definitely something underlying in Blanche's words and tone. As I stood there trying to think of a polite way to pry without annoying her, Blanche turned and focused on me. The way she stared made me think she didn't miss much; I felt totally transparent.

"You look melancholy, Tatum. Are you feeling down?"

I looked down at my body for the second time in ten

minutes, and tried to see what she saw. My silver, beat-up gladiator sandals were laced around my ankles. My bare legs, not nearly as toned as Tilly's, were thankfully tan, despite the fact I hadn't spent much time in the sun. Next, denim shorts, strategically frayed at the edges, and a plain black tank top. I wasn't trying to impress anybody. My chocolate-brown, shoulder-length hair was pushed back behind my ears, and I could feel my cheeks were flushed from the already-too-hot weather. I blinked at Blanche from behind the long lashes I'd been told I inherited from my mother. All in all, utterly forgettable, but melancholy? After the last several days, I supposed I ought to be, so maybe I was. I shrugged. "Maybe?"

She laughed. "At least you're honest. So tell me something. Why am I here?"

"Belén invited you?" I stammered.

"Yes, I'm aware of that, thank you, dear." Sarcasm on an old person was funny. "Why did she feel the need to invite me?"

I assumed Blanche already knew about my scandalous behavior, so I wondered why she was beating a dead horse. "Because she's thinks I need a babysitter, and you drew the short straw." It came out with more bite than I intended.

Luckily, she laughed again. "I wouldn't call it the short straw. I wouldn't have come if I didn't think it was worth my time."

Huh. So she thought this was a good way to spend her summer. Keeping watch over me. Curiouser and curiouser, this woman.

"I'm sure Belén told you all the gory details, so why do we need to rehash this?" I turned and started for the door, cheeks growing warmer, ashamed that another adult in my life was going to judge me, yet again, for something I didn't do. I'd had about enough of that lately.

Blanche reached out and put a cool hand on my wrist. Her flowery perfume tickled my nose. "I want to hear the story from you. I know my daughter can give a . . . biased, shall we say, account of things. What really happened?"

I paused for a minute, considering. I wasn't exactly in the mood to talk about my arrest for the millionth time, but something in the way she'd said "biased" made me doubt that Blanche was going to jump on the "Tatum is a juvenile delinquent" bandwagon.

My hesitation must have made her reconsider. She gripped my wrist a little more firmly, as if trying to send a signal. "Maybe now isn't the best time. When you're ready. And if you don't ever want to talk, that's okay too. But I'm a good listener."

She raised her eyebrows meaningfully and let go. Baffled that a relative of Belén's was actually going to let me make my own choice about something, I nodded and went to my room.

Abby emailed, asking again if she could give me credit for designing the logo on her website, which meant I needed to come up with a business name. Unlucky for me, being confined to the walls of our house the majority of my

day gave me a lot of time to think about that. And lots of
time to think meant I was lying faceup on my bed, staring at the ceiling, willing the design muse to take me.
Everything I came up with felt too silly or immature,
or just altogether not right. Anything that was a play on
design or computers or pixels felt just plain oblivious. I
wanted something special. Desperate, I started looking
around my room for inspiration.

Piles of jewelry and cosmetics sat on my dresser in a
haphazard fashion. Belén was forever nagging me to clean
it up.

"How can you find anything in this mess?" she'd say. I
ignored her tone. There was an art to my piles.

"I know exactly where everything is," I'd retort,
and she'd let it go. Until the next time she came into my
room, anyway.

The silver chains dangling small charms and the plain
hoop earrings didn't inspire me. My twelve beige eyeshad-
ows, neutral powders, and blushes didn't help any, either.
The posters on the wall were mostly black-and-white
photography, except for the print of Rene Magritte's *The
Blank Signature*. My dad took me to the National Gallery
when I was twelve, a special father-daughter date, and I
fell in love with surrealism. He bought me the print and
had it framed; it'd hung there ever since. I turned my eyes
to my desk, which held my laptop and an empty tea mug,
bearing the emblem of my dad's alma mater, Georgetown
University's School of Foreign Service. The tag from a
peppermint tea bag hung down the side, fluttering from
the ceiling fan whirring above me. Thinking about my

dad left a sinking sadness in the hollow of my throat, and I looked away.

My closet doors had been flung open that morning as I attempted to find the perfect outfit for staying inside and not soaking up the sunshine after school like the rest of my classmates. I glanced over my T-shirts and shorts, peppered with the occasional sundress or skirt, which hung neatly on their sturdy white plastic hangers, little soldiers ready to battle high school. No wire hangers allowed in Belén's house, thank you very much. And yet, still nothing jumped out.

I craned my neck to check out my nightstand, situated on the left side of my twin bed. My lamp was shaped like the Eiffel tower, and a stack of paperbacks sat next to it. And then, glinting in the afternoon light streaming through the window, were my keys. Correction: key. My sad and lonely house key, missing her car key sister, was attached to the only keychain I owned.

It wasn't really remarkable. If you were looking at keychains in a store, it wouldn't be the first one you picked up. Just a slim rectangle of silver metal with a plain silver ring punched through a hole at the end. It had the lyric "You'll never walk alone" stamped on it in flowery script, flanked by the outline of an angel wing on each side. My dad says that was the song played at my mother's funeral; I don't remember much about it, other than lots of crying. When I was seven, she'd wrapped her car around a tree after having one too many drinks at a charity event, losing the life she'd left us for three years prior.

Dad gave me the keychain, complete with brand-new

gold house key, when I was eleven, and he and Belén had deemed me responsible enough to let myself into the house after school. I knew I was moving up in the food chain only because no one was free to pick me up from school once Tilly started pointe classes, but I was happy for the extra independence just the same. My dad looked so pleased with himself when he presented it to me, saying he hoped it would remind me that even when I was home by myself, someone was always watching over me. That little strip of metal quickly became my worry stone, my rabbit's foot, my Xanax.

When I was sad or frustrated or feeling overwhelmed, I held it, rubbed my thumb over it, looked at it, and I was able to pull myself together, at least for a hot minute. The keychain didn't remind me of my mom so much—I mean, I barely remembered her—but the inscribed lyric made me hopeful. It made me feel that, despite all the doors that had closed on me along the way, a window could open at any time. I was still waiting for that window to show up. More than anything else, the keychain actually reminded me of my dad—my covert champion when no one else was. Would he still be that for me when he came home? I wasn't sure, and I didn't really want to imagine what it might be like if he wasn't.

I shoved those thoughts away and began contemplating the angel wings as a starting place for a logo. I pulled out my sketchbook—the one from that horrible day at Mason's, ironically—and messed around with different combinations of my name. The notebook kept reminding me of that fateful afternoon, though, which made me sad, until the lightbulb of inspiration went off.

At Mason's, when I'd handed the girl behind the counter my debit card to pay for the notebook and pencils, she'd looked at it, laughed, and said "TLC."

"Huh?" For a second, I'd thought she was going to break in song. Maybe bust out a little "No Scrubs" or "Waterfalls."

"Because *T* is your first initial, and Elsea is your last name. TLC. Get it?" I smiled politely and told her, yes, I got it.

For a company name, though, it might be memorable, and it didn't annoy me, so I doodled it between the wings. TLC Design. I studied my rough sketch and smiled, decided. That would work. Maybe there was a small, serendipitous silver lining to having been at the store that day after all. Perhaps I could make a thimbleful of lemonade with my gigantic pile of lemons.

I had an urge to pick up my phone and call my best friend to tell her I'd had a moment of brilliance, but that unfortunately wasn't an option at the moment. I smiled anyway, hoping that I'd get to giggle about this with Ash. And hoping it would happen soon.

I spent the rest of my evening online, gleefully putting my design and my new TLC Design email address on all kinds of swag, like business cards and pens. I drew the line at rubber bracelets, but bookmarked the link for later, just in case. I was about to enter my payment information for the stuff when I felt someone's presence behind me. I quickly tried to think of a lie that didn't sound like I'd just pulled it out of thin air. A school project was always safe. The warmth of whoever it was drew closer to my face, and I turned slowly. Instead of my cyborg stepmonster or ice queen stepsis, it was my new grandmother. Interesting. I watched her out of the corner of my eye, and decided to wait and see if she made the first move.

"Why do you need pens with the name of a singing group on them?" She cocked her head to the side, still checking out the screen on my laptop.

I snorted. "You know who TLC is?"

"I know a lot about music, Tatum. I don't live under a rock, you know."

I instantly looked down, chastised. "I didn't mean to imply . . . Sorry. I mean, well, most people your, um, age, aren't familiar with popular music from the last couple of decades. My dad, for example, still thinks Poison is cool because their lead singer has been on, like, twelve reality TV shows. Which in my world means they've hit rock bottom. But that's just me."

Blanche patiently waited for me to finish rambling. I shut my mouth, self-conscious, and let her speak. "The pens, Tatum?"

"Oh, right." I debated whether or not I should tell her the truth. She was Belén's mother, after all, but something about her made me think I could trust her. The hip-hop knowledge also didn't hurt. "I'm starting a freelance business, actually."

She smiled slyly. "How enterprising of you."

"My fine isn't going to pay itself."

"Fine?" She raised a dark, shapely eyebrow.

I narrowed my eyes suspiciously. She was a sneaky one. "I'm sure you know about that already."

She sat down on my unmade bed. "Yes, we've established that. And we also established that I'd prefer to hear about it from you."

I looked at the screen again, and then back to Blanche. Her face still held the kindness that had been there when she first arrived, and as I was feeling hopeful, and impulsive, I jumped. "Do you want the short version, or the long version?"

"Whatever you want to share." For such a tiny woman, she was a commanding presence. Her voice, though soft, had authority, and I didn't feel comfortable saying no to her. Her daughter could take a lesson on communication from her mother.

I sucked in a breath. "Well. My best friend, who may now be my *former* best friend, decided to date a complete creep who got arrested for grand larceny and decided to take the two of us along for the ride. I named names, I got a five-hundred-dollar fine, a misdemeanor charge, and community service. He's in jail, and she's sequestered at boarding school and won't speak to me."

Blanche looked me in the eyes the entire time I spoke, and I never saw any judgment pass through them. That was a small relief. Two more points to Blanche. "So. Yeah. Now I'm on house arrest. Oh, and my dad left the country still mad at me. There's that too."

She was quiet for a beat, and then nodded once. "And you've started a business of some sort to pay the fine?"

"Well, not exclusively, no. That was just good timing,

I guess. I make logos, headers, and such for websites, that kind of thing."

"You must be very talented if people are willing to pay for your work."

I frowned. "Only one person, so far. But hopefully more. And I don't know about talented. I'm just good with the software, I guess." The heartbreak of getting rejected from McIntosh still loomed over my head like a storm cloud threatening to break open and douse me. I knew I was a competent artist, but not making it into the most selective of high schools still hurt more than I wanted to admit.

"Did you make this logo for yourself?" Blanche gestured to the screen and my incomplete order.

"Yep." I looked at her and saw something I hadn't seen from my stepfamily recently, or maybe ever. Interest. "What, um, do you think of it?"

"It's simple, but effective. The wings are a nice touch, I think. Makes it seem like you'd care about your clients." She nodded again, approvingly. Huh. I just thought I was swiping from a keychain. "Do they mean anything?"

I looked away, not ready to share that much; I'd told her enough for one night.

She understood immediately, perceptive woman, and rose from the bed. "You'd better complete your order. Maybe you can leave some cards at Matilda's school later this week."

Tilly had an end-of-the-year extravaganza at McIntosh in a couple days. "I'd have to pay extra to get it here in time." And I didn't add that I barely had enough in my savings account to cover the swag.

Blanche held up one finger, as if to tell me to hold on for a second, and disappeared. When she came back moments later, she stepped toward me and slid something onto my desk, next to the laptop. A credit card. I looked up at her astonished, mouth gaping, too confused to speak.

"Put it back on my dresser when you're done. You can make it up to me later. And don't worry. I won't tell her." She winked and left.

It felt a little like I'd found myself a fairy godmother.

Chapter 4

The last day of school came and went without fanfare. Most of the buzz about me and Ashlyn had died down to a dull roar by then. It was such a wasted day, due to exams being over; most kids used the last few hours to write clichés in each other's yearbooks about how that person magically changed their lives that year, or how they hoped to see them at the pool. I might have been guilty of the same meaningless words if I'd had someone to say them to. Like Ashlyn. Instead, I just wished my classmates a nice summer and left it at that. I didn't really have the energy for anything more creative.

Driving home, my phone rang. I let it go to voicemail, and at the next red light quickly put on the Bluetooth and checked the caller. Mrs. Schmidt, my favorite babysitting client. I smiled and immediately called her back.

"Oh, hi, Tatum," she said brightly in my left ear.

"Thanks for calling back so quickly. Did you listen to my message?"

"Hi, Mrs. Schmidt. Nope, I'm driving. I figured calling back was easier."

"Well, I have some bad news and some good news." I didn't think anything she had to tell me could make my life worse.

"All right. Give me the bad news first."

"The bad news is that, sadly, we won't be needing your babysitting services this summer."

My jaw dropped open. I had watched the Schmidt girls, Maya and Kate, for the last three years, while Mrs. Schmidt worked from home. She was a freelance editor for a women's magazine and always had a hard time staying on schedule when the girls were underfoot.

"Oh. Okay," I said quietly. Had I done something? Had she heard about my legal mishap?

"My husband's grandmother passed away, and we inherited her home on the Eastern Shore. We're all going to spend the summer there, if you can believe it. We haven't had a family vacation in years, so this is really a gift." Phew. I was sad for their loss, but selfishly glad their change in plans had nothing to do with me.

"That's amazing. Congratulations." They were a hard-working family and definitely deserved the break.

"Thanks, hon. So here's the good news. We would love to hire you as a pet sitter instead."

"No vacation for the critters?"

"My sister-in-law and her kids are coming too, and her youngest is allergic to pretty much anything that's not human, so the pets are staying at home." Maya had picked out a hamster named Princess Sweetheart on her fifth birthday last year, and Kate had the fourth in a long line of beta fish, Mr. Blue. There was also a very overweight gray cat named Gus. Despite his grumpy demeanor, Gus was an excellent sport, having been subjected to countless hours of dress-up and tea parties with the girls. "So, do you think you can handle taking care of our zoo?"

I laughed. "Sure, I think I can manage."

She clapped her hands, the sound smacking in my ear. "Excellent. I think a couple times a week will be fine, and you know where the food is. You can work around your schedule, as I'm sure you have a lot of exciting plans. Start next Monday?"

Little did she know, and I wasn't going to tell her any differently about my so-called *exciting plans.* "You can count on me. Have a great time. Give the girls a hug for me."

"I will. Thanks, Tatum, you're a lifesaver." She disconnected.

Although pet sitting hadn't been part of the plan, I thought that maybe it could be for the best. An empty house at my disposal all summer, with no scary Belén checking up on me? That could work out nicely after all.

My first official summer outing under Belén's reign was pretty much how I would describe torture. McIntosh, being the school for special snowflakes, held a monumental final performance-slash-exhibition-slash-culminating gala-slash-evening of celebration for its students. Which felt like a huge slap in the face by artistic professionals, showing me the kind of work I'd never be capable of matching, since they'd rejected me two years ago. I'd balked when Belén brought it up at the breakfast table, but she'd put her foot down.

"Tatum, we're going to show support for your sister."

I really wanted to protest that A), Tilly was my stepsister, emphasis on the *step*, and B), didn't forcing me to go kind of cancel out the whole support thing? I always thought support was something you gave freely, without coercion, but maybe that was just me. Then again, I reminded myself I had my own client-finding agenda, and brightened.

"Is Blanche going?" I asked hopefully. She'd mentioned it at our "secret" meeting the other night. Maybe she and I could walk around the exhibits together.

"No, she has something else on her social calendar."

I glanced over at Blanche, who was busy stirring her honey-flavored Greek yogurt. "I just feel awful, but it couldn't be rescheduled. My old friend Carolina is leaving town tomorrow and won't be back until after I've gone home. I made plans to have dinner with her the moment I knew I was coming to Virginia. Matilda understands, and she's already said she would show me the video of tonight's performance later on." Blanche smiled warmly at her granddaughter and stirred once more. She took a bite and looked pointedly at my stepmother. "I have already, I might point out, purchased our tickets for Matilda's culminating performance with her dance company. No shaming from you." Another score for Blanche.

I'd have to go it alone then. I reminded myself that this was the very last item on the end-of-school checklist before I morphed into "girl with no life." And by no life, I meant I would be serving my hours, hopefully painlessly, and earning money via my new business and pet sitting. I was fairly sure I could make it through tonight, even without Blanche to entertain me.

"Oh," I said absently, remembering my swag was supposed to arrive that day. "If a delivery truck comes with something for me, can you let me know right away? Please?"

Belén and Tilly looked up from sipping their coffee, in unison, and Belén's deep-brown eyes narrowed, either out of curiosity or suspicion. Probably the latter.

"You're expecting a package, Tatum?"

Crud. "Yes." I willed myself to think of something she wouldn't question. "It's a college guide. One of those really thick ones. Jam-packed with statistics."

Belén nodded in approval. "The truck usually comes before noon."

"Great," I said, and sipped my tea so I wouldn't be compelled to say anything else. I couldn't wait to see how the pens turned out, and smiled to myself at the thought of things coming together.

After a long day researching various community service options, I sat down to an uncomfortable dinner, where I was forced to listen to Belén and Tilly go through every

teeny step of the dance routine Tilly would be performing that evening, and the matching facial expressions. Just
before we got in the car and made our way to the school,
I stuffed my purse with express-shipped TLC business
cards and pens, complete with angel wing logo. I had
beaten everyone else to the front door when the truck
pulled up, and practically launched myself at the poor,
unsuspecting delivery guy. To my amazement, the promo
items had come out far better than I could have imagined.
I felt very professional, knowing my swag could get me
real, paying clients so I could finish off that ludicrous fine
before September. And, in my more optimistic moments,
I dreamed I might get that tablet after all. I spent the ride
thinking of ways to discretely leave my cards and pens
about, my fingers idly stroking the smooth metal of the
keychain in my pocket.

As soon as we entered the school, Belén and Tilly
vanished. I wasn't sure what time Tilly was scheduled to
perform over the course of the evening; I just assumed she
went off somewhere to warm up, and Belén was either
planning to hover over her or meet up with the other helicopter parents to gush over their perfect children. It was
just as well. I didn't think either of them would register
my presence in the audience, so I strolled around the other
exhibits instead of spending my energy to find out where
and when Tilly was dancing.

The art on display was in the cafeteria on large port-
able partitions and the walls. Like all school cafeterias,
the smell of stale french fries permeated the air, and I
wrinkled my nose. The whole setup took me back to the

very first time one of my own pieces was in an art show. I was ten, and so terrified that Belén had stuffed a paper bag into her purse for fear I'd hyperventilate before we got to the art studio. While she and my dad walked around the displays and checked out all the artwork, I made a beeline right to my painting. It was the century-old carousel from Glen Echo Park, in watercolors. My dad and Belén had taken Tilly and me there one spring afternoon when the light made the colors on the old wooden horses practically shimmer. They'd walked around; I'd sketched. When I approached my piece, I noticed two ribbons lying on the ground nearby—one red and one blue. Which one was mine? My little heart sped up, hoping against hope that the blue one was for me. First place. My dad and Belén would be so proud of me.

I picked up both ribbons and, without thinking twice, stuck the blue one to my painting and the red one to the pastel drawing next to it. I stood there with perma-grin, waiting for my dad and Belén to make their way over. Which they did. With a judge right behind them. I blocked out much of the conversation that followed, but I specifically remember feeling small and confused. I was only trying to do what Belén had told me to do—do my best. First place was best, right? My dad took me aside, explained that the better choice would have been to ask the judge which ribbon belonged with which painting, and then ushered me over to said judge to apologize. The photograph of me and all the other elementary-school artists, rightful red ribbon in hand and red eyes looking at the floor, used to sit, framed, on the mantle at home.

I may or may not have been responsible for hiding it in a drawer, never to be seen again.

With a sigh and a quick glance around the room, I spied my target. A long folding table was set up near the far exit, covered in what looked like brochures and program literature. Bingo. I crossed quickly, on a mission, and stepped up in front of the woman, a McIntosh parent I assumed, plastering a confident smile on my face.

"Hi there, ma'am," I said through my grin, and waited for her to look up.

"Yes, dear, how can I help you? Can I interest you in next month's trip to Italy?"

Who wouldn't be interested? I accepted the flyer she handed me and practically drooled over the amazing photograph of the Ponte Vecchio positioned front and center. I doused that flame and shook my head. "Unfortunately, I'm booked solid all summer. My loss."

The lady put on a fake pout and then raised her eyebrows, waiting to find out why I was standing in front of her. "Actually, I'm hoping you wouldn't mind if I leave some business cards and pens here for students to pick up. I recently launched a graphic design company, and thought some McIntosh students might find my services useful. For websites and portfolios."

Her eyes narrowed. "So you aren't a student here, then?"

I shook my head again. "No, I go to Henderson. My sister goes here though. She suggested I advertise here tonight." A little white lie, but who knows, maybe Tilly would have encouraged my plans. Not that I would have told her. I gave the lady my best innocent face, my eyes wide and lip on the verge of trembling. "So is it okay?"

I was just about to up the ante and bat my eyelashes when she nodded, lips pursed in a line.

"I suppose it would be fine. I'm sure there are plenty of students looking for help with portfolios for college applications."

I smiled and hauled the stuff out of my bag before she could change her mind or I could lose my nerve. It still didn't sit well that I was keeping my graphic design business a secret from my dad, but he wasn't here to tell anyway, and I definitely wasn't going to tell Belén. I'd always felt she looked down her nose at my art, thought of it as favorable to something like 4-H but definitely not as good for my résumé as violin or tennis. I was perfectly happy allowing her to believe the Schmidts were paying me excessively to watch Maya and Kate. I arranged the business cards in a fan design and laid a small pile of pens horizontally at the base of the fan.

The woman picked up a card. "Well, aren't these darling? I love the angel wings."

"Thank you."

"And TLC, that is just precious. Tender Loving Care, am I right?" Well, at least she didn't reference the singing group.

"No, ma'am. It's actually a play on my name."

She inspected the card closer, looking for my name, which I'd left off to avoid my family catching on, and to also steer clear of any weirdos who might randomly find my site. "Ah. You said you do websites?"

"Yes, ma'am. And graphic design."

She nodded and tucked my card into the back pocket of her mom jeans. "My daughter is just finishing ninth grade, but I'm going to keep you in mind for next year."

I gave her that winning smile again. "Thank you very much. I'll look forward to working with her." I offered my hand to shake; it seemed like the right thing to do. She took it and shook it firmly.

"Nice to meet you, Miss TLC."

"You too." I gave her a little wave and walked away. At least I'd impressed one person.

I meandered aimlessly through the exhibits and found myself standing in front of a wall decorated with student-made event posters. They boasted things like poetry coffee houses, school plays, and concerts. Little placards were posted underneath, sporting a different name from the ones displayed on the posters. The artists. My face burned with jealousy. They were beautiful reminders of how much better my own work might have been at this point if I'd benefitted from the amazing teachers here. And yet, like a train wreck, I couldn't stop looking, wishing I had something on display for all to see. Wishing I wasn't forced to be at McIntosh to see all I missed out on. Wishing I wasn't going to be missing out on even more this summer. Wishing things were different in a lot of ways.

I wish, I wish, I wish.

Anger rose in my chest, threatening to spill out in a scream, but I muffled it with a clamped jaw. With clenched fists, I slid along the wall of posters, the bright colors and swirly scripts blurring before my eyes.

"What do you think of that one?" I jerked my head to the left, surprised to find someone standing next to me. My eyes landed on a pair of green ones, the same color as sea glass. I blinked a couple of times before I realized he had asked me a question.

"I'm sorry, what?" I looked away quickly, my cheeks flushing with embarrassment.

He laughed, soft and low. "You okay there? I just asked what you thought of the poster."

I jerked my head to where he was gesturing. The advertisement was for the jazz ensemble's holiday concert, created by someone named Summer Smith. The gold font was big and showy, glittering like the photographs of the instruments themselves. Sparse snowflakes dotted the border. I nodded slowly.

"It's nice work. There's a definite theme, and it feels like a true collaboration between the artist and the musicians." I smiled at my shoes.

"You have a good eye. One of my friends plays the trombone for that group; they worked for a week batting ideas back and forth with the designer." The guy pointed to the next poster on the right. "And this one?"

I lifted my head and inspected it. This poster, by James Williams, wanted the viewer to attend a solo cello recital. It was stark—white with a black, androgynous stick figure and an outline of a cello between its straight-line legs.

The spare words simply listed a time and place, and the name of the performer, Seamus Kipsang.

Frowning, I cocked my head to the side. "What kind of name is that? Wasn't he Harry Potter's friend?"

A musical laugh came from beside me. I shifted my eyes and took a minute to look him over. Wow. Maybe I should have done that first. The bright-green eyes were attached to a face with the most flawlessly perfect skin I'd ever seen—an exact match with *tawny brown* on Pantone's color palette. He stood half a head taller than me, and his cheekbones gave John Legend a run for his money. I shoved my hands into the pockets of my dress, the warm metal in my right hand calming my nerves.

His left eyebrow lifted. "So, the poster? What are your thoughts?"

I managed to collect myself long enough to look back at the poster and consider the actual picture. "Right. It's okay. A little boring. I might have added a little color somewhere. Maybe the performer's name in red or something. I dunno, it doesn't really move me. Or tell me anything about the performer. Honestly, it doesn't make me want to go to the show."

"Brutal," he said, laughing. I shrugged, and the guy nodded. "Yeah, color would definitely make it stand out more."

"Right? You want people to notice you and come to your performance." I pointed to the poster to the right of the black-and-white one, this time for a duet ballet performance by Graham Lund and So Jung Ha. "Take that one. What jumps out at you?"

He turned and looked at it thoughtfully. "The definition in her muscles." The designer had used a blue-and-white photograph of the female dancer's neck and collarbone, only adding a small amount of script across the top and the bottom so the viewer's eye was drawn immediately to the picture.

"Exactly. The lines are phenomenal, and definitely make me think of power and strength, which is what dancing is all about, right?" I knew that much from watching Tilly for so many years. I checked out the designer's name. "If Radhika Vij was here, I would shake her hand."

The guy fumbled with his pockets and pulled out a tiny notebook, similar to the one Abby always had with her. His face took on a panicked look, brows knitted together in a straight line. He patted the pocket at his chest and gave up, sighing. "You don't have a pen, do you? I want to write down what you just said."

"Are you a reporter or something?" I quirked an eyebrow up, unsure if being quoted in the *McIntosh Musings* was a good idea for my anonymity.

He shook his head adamantly. His dark hair, closely cropped to his head, had a tight curl running through it. "No, no, not a chance. I'm crap at research. I liked your comments and didn't want to forget them. They make sense to me."

Before I could decide if he was for real or just handing me a line, I blushed. I'm not a blusher normally, but there was something in the way he said it, something honest, that made my cheeks light up. To distract myself, I stuck my hand down into the pocket of my messenger bag and came up with a lone pen that somehow hadn't made it onto the table earlier. I handed it to him without looking at his face. "Here."

He took it, and about a millimeter of my skin brushed against his, but it was enough to send a shiver of electricity up my arm. I jerked my arm back in shock, and maybe a little bit from fear of being so close to him—not that I'd admit that out loud. He looked up when I took my arm away, and confusion flashed in his eyes, now brighter with emotion. "Sorry," he mumbled, and I blushed again, this time from embarrassment.

"No, I was, I mean, you, er . . . Oh, crud." I trailed off, wishing I could cover myself with the performance posters and fade into the wall. He didn't seem to notice my bumbling, as he was scribbling furiously in the notebook. I glanced over and saw my thoughts, word for word, entwined with his own. I looked a little more closely and read them aloud.

"Close up of body, maybe bow, rosin dust on the fingers," I read slowly. "These are your notes to the artist?"

He nodded. "Kind of. I'm getting a jumpstart on my summer assignment for senior English. Due first day of school in the fall." He looked at me quizzically. "Which you would know if you went here."

I shrugged. "Just along for the ride today, I'm afraid."

He nodded, and we moved on. We walked slowly, pausing at each piece of artwork, each installation, each small flat-screen broadcasting a clip of a performance. He asked my opinions and I gave them openly. I noticed as I spoke that he always looked me in the eye, always stayed in the moment with me, didn't allow himself to be distracted by the people around us. If I was being honest with myself, he looked at me like I was actually there, which for me was a nice change of pace from feeling like persona non grata lately. It was also nice to have an intelligent conversation, or actually any conversation, that didn't involve me being scolded or made to feel like the planet's biggest human disappointment. I tried to keep the smiling to a minimum, so to not scare him off with my megawattage. I was enjoying myself so much that I didn't even realize the guy had stopped walking; like inertia, I kept on moving, and my face met his chest. Like a brick wall.

"Ooof." I stumbled backward less than gracefully, rubbing my nose. As I tried, unsuccessfully, to regain my balance, thrown off not only by the collision but by the rock hardness of his pectoral muscles, a pair of even stronger hands gripped my forearms and held me steady.

"You all right?" He released me gently once I was stable.

"Oh sure, nothing wounded but my pride." I gave him a tight-lipped smile and crossed my arms, attempting to seem nonchalant, unfazed, when in reality every bone in my body was screaming to abort the mission. I scanned the room and noted Belén standing off to the side, phone attached to her fingers. "Hey, uh, I should probably get going, I see my ride looking like she's had enough art for one night." No need to mention who I was here with. He might have class with Tilly, and if he did, he might know about me, and frankly, I was content to leave things as they were. Better to be the semi-interesting girl who knows a little bit about aesthetics than Tilly's black-sheep stepsister.

When I looked up, his eyes completely focused on me like no one else was in the room, I thought I detected something like disappointment on his face. He blinked it away and smiled, then handed the pen back and closed his notebook, holding it behind his back.

"Well, it was really nice talking to you. Refreshing, actually."

This surprised me. "How do you mean?"

"Everyone around here is so caught up in themselves and trying to be the best. So they humor you and compliment your work, even if it sucks, because they're afraid you might turn around and be just as honest with them. Artists have fragile egos, it seems."

I put a hand on my hip and arched an eyebrow. "And you don't?" I wondered what kind of artist he was.

He laughed out loud. "Oh, I have my moments of uncertainty." At least he had a sense of humor about it. "It was nice to talk to a girl who isn't afraid to say what's on her mind. I appreciated the honesty."

I snorted. It did not escape me that this random guy who didn't know me from Adam thought I was great for doing exactly the thing my best friend hated me for— telling the truth. He tipped his head to the side, confused, and I replaced my smirk with a smile.

"Thanks for that, it's nice to hear." And I meant it. He just didn't know how much or why.

I felt a chill and realized Belén was glaring at me, her almost-black eyes threatening to march herself over here and remind me that I was still being punished, which I'm sure meant no chatting with cute boys and looking like I was having fun of any kind.

I sighed. "I really need to go. It was nice talking to you too."

Before he could say anything else—and I'm guessing he wanted to, since his jaw unhinged like he was getting ready to speak—I turned on my heels and fled the hall, then went out the front door and to the car. As I leaned against the rear passenger door and waited for Belén and Tilly to come back, I pulled out my phone and settled my weight on one foot, flipping through my contact list for someone to text with. When I scrolled past Ashlyn's name, I clicked the power button and slid the phone back into my purse, then closed my eyes, wishing for something I knew wasn't coming.

Chapter 5

I didn't leave the house again until Monday morning. The rest of my weekend was spent obsessively checking my email, telling myself that a potential client might reach out, but really, I knew I was waiting to see if Ashlyn would reply. She didn't.

The first day of community service with the Arlington Parks Authority brought ninety-degree sunshine with it. I'd finally chosen to spend my summer days removing invasive plants from the city's numerous parks because, let's be honest, it was the activity I thought would invite the least amount of conversation from Belén. I also thought—very maturely, I might add, and maybe masochistically—that a little manual labor might be good for me. Builds character, as adults like to say when they really just want kids to do their dirty work. And, I also didn't think it would hurt my college applications to say I'd "interned" with the park service on a "botany project." I was nothing if not forward thinking.

I was the first one down to breakfast that day, since I had to be up at the crack of dawn, and was just finishing up my bowl of apples and cinnamon oatmeal when Tilly came down the stairs, practically skipping, brand-new toe shoes in hand. When she saw me sitting at the table, the tranquil smile that had graced her face slipped into a half frown. I could see her warring with herself over whether or not to be pleasant or frigid.

"Good morning," I said loudly. She paused on her way to the cabinet and offered me a faint smile, but it didn't make it to her eyes.

Tilly was tall and willowy, just like her mother. She had the same warm, glowing skin and the same thick black hair, though Tilly's was shot through with red when the light hit just right. She seemed slight, but I knew that her frame packed a lot more muscle than was obvious to the casual observer. Though I'd never tell her out loud, I admired her for her grit. Dancing was not a sport for the weak. I'd seen her feet bruised, cracked, and bleeding on a regular basis, and yet she kept on going. Just as regularly, I was glad graphic design was an indoor, sedentary activity. As Tilly sat down at the table and began the grueling process of cutting and stretching her toe shoes to make them conform to her feet better, I wondered if I'd made a mistake by choosing to spend a whole one hundred hours hunched over, pulling plants out of the ground. Was I punishing myself even further?

"So," I began, making an awkward attempt at conversation.

Tilly didn't look up from her task or respond. I didn't bother trying again.

Belén came clacking down the stairs in her three-inch heels and tailored skirt and blazer. White pearls, black hair, white blouse, black suit. She was a study in monochromatics. When she reached the table, she wordlessly handed me my car key, which looked naked without its usual partner. I instinctively stuck my hand in my shorts pocket—utilitarian khaki had seemed appropriate for cutting down vines in the jungle, which is how I pictured my day going—and came up empty. I patted my hips, but only felt skin and muscle beneath. My heart rate picked up as I glanced frantically around the kitchen. Where was my keychain?

Like a mind reader, Belén raised an eyebrow and put a hand on her hip, her pointy elbow ready to impale. "You lost your key?"

"I'm sure it's here somewhere," I said, rising to go search my room.

"You'll have to look for it later, Tatum. You can't add being late on top of everything else on your first day on the job." The disappointment in her voice had turned to judgment, as she'd slowly extended the "everything else."

I couldn't look at her, and my ears started burning with shame.

"Thanks for the vote of confidence." I grabbed my shoulder bag and slid my feet into my weathered sneakers. Belén fished a color-coded and labeled house key out of the spare key drawer (because why wouldn't you have a drawer specifically for spare keys), handed it over, and nodded toward the garage door.

"Go."

Tilly never once looked up from her toe shoes during the entire embarrassing exchange. And why would she? We weren't the type of siblings to defend each other.

I opened the garage door and got into the car, shoving the key into the ignition. I racked my brain trying to think of where my missing keychain might be, retraced my steps to the last time I'd had it. I realized I hadn't actually left my room, let alone the house, except for the bathroom and meals, since Friday night when we went to the showcase at McIntosh. I smacked my forehead in frustration, a little too hard. The keychain must have fallen out of my pocket when I was walking around the school. I closed my eyes and sat there, letting the car idle, willing myself not to cry.

That keychain was long gone now, probably picked up by a janitor after the event. I didn't care about the house key, as it could be replaced easily, but that solid, unassuming strip of silver, stamped with its calming message, was breaking my heart. Salty tears pricked the corners of my eyes, and I rubbed them away furiously. No. I would not let this beat me. I told myself that it didn't matter, it was just keychain that meant nothing, and backed out of the garage, my chest heaving and my lungs gasping for air.

The ten-minute drive to the park service headquarters did nothing to calm me. My heart raced and thoughts of crashing—accidentally—into trees and guardrails invaded my mind as I drove, fearing that without my little bit of luck on a chain, horrible things would happen. As I pulled into a place in front of the plain, brick building, I laughed. Why did I think a car accident was worse than alienating my friend, getting a criminal record, being on house arrest, and losing my father's trust? The keychain hadn't stopped those things from happening. My luck had already run out.

I focused on the green letters on the building, *Arlington Parks Authority*, wishing with all my might that this might be a chance to prove myself. To myself and no one else.

I followed the signs that said "Orientation" down a short hallway and into a large conference room, taking one of the twelve seats around an oval table. The only other person there was a guy I recognized from school. Hunter Hansen was in my grade at school, and was best known for being in a band. I'd had a class or two with him over the years, but we weren't friends. He always seemed a little aloof in that "I'm a musician" way that's both annoying and alluring. Hunter's dark blond hair was on the long side, grazing the tops of his ears in a manner I knew Belén would never approve of, and he wore a Ramones T-shirt and black jeans. It was the stereotypical "boy in a band" uniform. I wondered why he was electing to pull plants on his summer vacation.

"Hey, Hunter," I said, with a small wave. Might as well be friendly if we were going to be working together.

"Tatum." He just nodded.

"So what're you in for?" I laughed at my own joke, quite sure he hadn't been court ordered to this.

"Um, college applications. I like plants, did really well

in bio class. My counselor thought I needed some service on my résumé, so here I am. You?"

No use in lying about it. He probably already knew anyway and was just being polite. "The commonwealth attorney thought I needed some service on my criminal résumé."

"No kidding? Huh. I heard something about Ashlyn Zanotti getting in trouble, but never would've thought you were involved."

I sighed. "Thanks for thinking that, because I wasn't actually involved. I happened to be in the wrong place at the wrong time with the very wrong people." I sat down in my chair, feeling somewhat vindicated that Hunter had thought the best of me.

"It happens," he said, and shrugged like it was no big deal. Amazing. My impression of Hunter went up a few notches for his lack of judgment.

A couple more kids filed in, and we all stared at the ceiling silently, waiting for whoever was in charge to hurry up and get this party started. Just when the awkward silence was building to a frenzy, for me anyway, a tall, earthy-crunchy woman in a parks authority T-shirt and hiking boots appeared in the doorway. She seemed to be counting us.

"Hi, everyone, my name is Alicia Tilner. I'll be your supervisor this summer on the Invasive Plant Removal Team. Looks like we're waiting for just one more. Is everyone in the right place?"

"I definitely am," I said loudly. Hunter snorted. The other kids looked up, surprised at my faux enthusiasm. One or two laughed.

"Oh, excuse me, I think I'm supposed to be in here," came a voice from behind Alicia. My one and only client, Abby Gold herself, stood there, waiting to be let through the door.

"You're late." Alicia eyed her warily. I made a mental note to heed Belén's advice and always be on time for this shindig. Abby gave Alicia an apologetic smile and pushed into the room. She saw me and her smile widened, her eyes crinkling. I returned it, happy to have an ally.

"Right, so again, this is the IPRT. I'll be your supervisor and will be showing you what you're going to be doing. It's fairly simple—you just need to know what you're looking for." Alicia flicked on a projector that lit up a large screen on the far wall, and clicked through photographs of the invasive plants we'd need to be on the lookout for. "The biggest perpetrators"—I flinched at the term—"are sometimes the prettiest. This summer we're looking to take out English ivy and honeysuckle."

Abby raised her hand, but didn't wait to be called on. "Honeysuckle? Really? But it smells so good."

Hunter laughed and chimed in. "And tastes good too. How can it be bad? Eating honeysuckle in the summertime is like a rite of passage around here."

I shuddered, recalling a time when I'd stuck my tongue on the tiny drop of liquid from a honeysuckle blossom, one of the few things my mother had taught me to do. Belén had brushed it out of my hand so forcefully, you'd have thought it was poison, saying it wasn't good for me to eat it. Terrified of ending up in the hospital with some scary honeysuckle disease, I'd never done it again.

"Right!" Abby offered Hunter her fist to bump across the table, and he knocked his with hers. Alicia's face stiffened.

"Let's take this seriously, okay? Invasive plants suck up the resources needed by native plants to survive and maintain our local ecosystem." She went back to her slides, and when she was done, she turned to face us once again. "You'll be in teams of two; we rely on the buddy system." She quickly divided us up, and I found myself, thankfully, paired with Abby. Hunter got stuck with a tiny boy, probably a middle schooler, who kept sneezing. Alicia led us out of the building and out into the "backyard," which was one of the city's larger parks. I squinted at the vast field bordered by patches of forest, and spotted a huge swath of honeysuckle along the tree line right away.

Alicia rolled a large wheelbarrow behind her, stacked with handheld pruning tools, gloves, and a gigantic box of plastic garbage bags. When I saw how small some of the tools were in comparison to the enormous plants I knew I'd be working on, my heart sank. Why couldn't I have picked the animal shelter?

Abby nudged me. "At least we'll be getting a tan, right?" I looked at her pale skin dotted with freckles and held my arms up to hers. I was at least three shades darker. Abby chuckled. "Or maybe not."

Alicia cleared her throat, and we stopped talking. "Grab a tool, some gloves, and a bag and get going. Make sure you're clipping the branches as close to the root as you can get. Try not to remove anything other than what we discussed. Ivy and honeysuckle. If you're not sure,

come find me, and I'll identify it for you. Questions?"
No one raised a hand. We were all too intimidated to say
anything. "Okay, go for it. Have fun!"

I scoffed. "Right." Abby and I took off in the direction of the honeysuckle I'd spotted, the sweat already
forming in my elbow creases and on the back of my neck.
"So, why exactly are you here?"

"Because it looks good on my college applications."
She didn't sound convinced.

"Really? You're a columnist in our award-winning
school newspaper, you're in, like, a million AP classes, and
you're about to launch your own website. I don't think
you need this."

She gave me a guilty look and then leaned in close,
not that any of the other pairs were near enough to hear
us. "Truth? You know Hunter Hansen?"

I looked over to where Hunter and his partner had
landed, in front of a large tree covered in ivy. "Yeah, I
know Hunter." Abby's cheeks flamed, and I connected the
dots. "Oooooh, you like him?"

"It's so embarrassing, but I couldn't stop myself. We
were in AP Bio together, and I may have been carrying
on about saving the environment, and he told me about
this project, and before I knew what I was doing, I'd
put my name on the list." She covered her face with her
gloved hands. "Totally mortifying, right?"

I laughed. "It's not any worse than being ordered by
the courts."

Hands still on her face, Abby's blue eyes peeked out
through spread fingers. "Right. I forgot. You didn't have

a choice, though. I did. That's way worse." I wasn't going to argue with her that I had, in fact, chosen this particular activity. "So. Since we have all this time and you have my undivided attention, do you want to talk about it?"

Obviously I knew what *it* was, but I wondered exactly how much Abby knew, what she thought *it* was. I subconsciously stuck a hand in my pocket to stroke my keychain and came up empty. I gulped. The anger and frustration from the day at Mason's was still fresh in my mind, Ashlyn's silence heavy in my chest, and I didn't want to waste this time out of my prison cell talking about what got me there. "Maybe later. I'd rather talk about Hunter." I grinned wickedly at her, and she covered her face again and moaned.

"I'm pathetic! But, Tatum, he's so great. The bad part is, I don't think he thinks of me as more than a friend. We met working on the paper together."

"I thought he was in a band."

"He is. He writes music reviews for us. So, me with my movie reviews and him with his concerts and albums, we end up working late nights together on our layouts, and, honest to goodness, I would sit there and move copy around with him until the sun rises."

I chuckled and snapped a particularly long branch, shoving it into my black garbage bag. "You've got it bad, girl."

Abby gathered up the small pile of branches she'd been collecting at her feet. "I know. It's a sickness."

"So how do you know he doesn't feel the same? Have you ever asked him?"

She shook her head. "I think I prefer to just fantasize about him fantasizing about me, perhaps on a stage or in a botanical garden, instead of thinking about possible rejection." She shook her head again and looked down at her feet. "I'm tragic."

I put a hand on her shoulder, her bare skin warm under the pink canvas of my gloves. "No, you definitely are not. Do you want to hear tragic?"

"Yes, please."

I took a deep breath. "I went to my stepsister's school the other night, for this showcase thing, and I bumped into a guy. Literally, actually, which hurt because his pecs were like granite. And he was amazing, though probably not as amazing as Hunter." I looked at her pointedly, and she laughed. "But amazing nonetheless. Smart, thoughtful, funny. We talked for a long time about art and color and emotions, and—are you ready for this—I didn't even tell him my name."

Abby's eyes went wide. "Seriously? Did he tell you his?"

"No! I think he wanted to, but I freaked and left before he could. The only thing I know about him is that he's a student at McIntosh. And he's hot."

It was Abby's turn to grasp my shoulder in solidarity. "We should start a club."

"The loser club?"

"How about the Missed Opportunities Club?"

My heart stopped for a second when she spoke the words. Abby didn't know how ridiculously perfect that name was, so I just nodded in agreement. *That is my life*, I thought. *A series of missed opportunities.*

I sucked in a breath and tried to play it off without Abby noticing my discomfort. "Exactly. Except, you have a golden opportunity right now, this very minute, which you set up yourself, so it'll only be missed if you don't get your scaredy-cat self together and do something."

Abby jammed the pile of branches at her feet into the garbage bag and stood up, squaring her shoulders and puffing her chest up confidently. "You're right. I will definitely do something. What, I'm not sure, but it'll be something." She looked across the field to where Hunter and his partner, sneezing away, were carting two completely full garbage bags back toward Alicia's wheelbarrow. "Tomorrow."

"What? Why not after our shift is over?"

Abby's shoulders tipped forward, a little defeated. "I'm not ready today. Just, uh, yeah, tomorrow," she said, looking at Hunter longingly.

"Yep, tragic."

Abby suddenly brightened. "All right, Tatum, I'll make you a deal. By the end of the summer, you and I will have taken control of our missed opportunities with an abundance of intestinal fortitude."

If I'd had a drink in my mouth, I would have spit it out all over her. I cocked my head to the side and clipped another branch. "Easier for you, remember? You know your crush's name."

She waved her hands in the air, brushing me off. "I didn't mean the guy you met. I was talking about Ashlyn."

I glanced down at my feet, planted on the brittle,

dead grass that had been overwhelmed by the horrid heat. "I didn't say anything about a missed opportunity with Ashlyn."

I lifted my gaze, and Abby looked me square in the eyes, which was both intimidating and heartwarming. I felt like she could see right through me, through my fake bravery act, my pretending I didn't care, that I wasn't hurt. "You didn't have to."

I looked away and pressed my mouth into a firm little line. We chattered amiably for the rest of our shift. By the time Alicia blew her silver whistle and called us back to the clearing, we'd filled six garbage bags full of branches and leaves. I looked back at the honeysuckle we'd been working on, and my heart fell into my stomach as I realized that even though we'd been cutting and stuffing for hours, we'd only just begun.

Chapter 6

When I got home, dirty and exhausted, I hopped right into the shower and stayed there for a solid twenty minutes. The hot water running over my aching shoulders provided a small shred of relief, albeit only physical. My conversation with Abby made me both sad and hopeful at the same time. I was grateful to have someone to talk to again, but that connection also scared me. She could become just one more person who'd end up disappointed in me. I didn't know if it was worth it to let her in, to trust her, but a little part of me thought it might be.

A loud banging came at the door. "Tatum! Mom says you need to come out of there." For a quiet girl, Tilly sure could yell.

I gritted my teeth, not ready to leave the warmth and solitude of the shower yet. "In a minute!"

She banged again. "Mom says you're wasting water!"

A snarky retort was on the tip of my tongue, but I bit it back. I counted to ten, slower than a tortoise, and shut the water off. I toweled dry and slid on a loose tank and worn pajama pants. The soft fabric felt fantastic on my tired and slightly crispy skin. I reminded myself to throw a higher SPF sunscreen in my bag for next time. Belén had lots of expensive tubes of 50 and higher stashed in her bathroom. I hung up my towel, opened the door, and smacked right into Tilly. Why was she still out there?

"Sorry," I mumbled, not totally meaning it. I shoved past her and made it almost all the way to my room before she called out in a sing-songy voice, "Mom says you have to come down to dinner tonight."

After my long day, the last thing I wanted was a dinner filled with awkward conversation and Belén's opinions on everything. I'd been looking forward to some peace and quiet. "What if I'm not hungry?"

She raised an eyebrow. "I think you know she's capable of dragging you down there, so you might as well just submit."

As much as I didn't want to admit it, she was right. I would not want to meet Belén in a dark alley. If she was paired up against a gang member in a street fight, my money would be on the pretty Chilean woman every time. Tilly marched down the stairs, never letting go of her dancer's posture, and I followed behind her reluctantly.

Blanche was putting a large bowl of porotos con riendas—bean and pasta stew—on the table when we arrived. I inhaled deeply, the savory scent making my stomach rumble. It smelled more delicious than the last time we'd had it; I wondered if Blanche had made it instead of Belén. I was grateful that one third of the company, as well as the food, wouldn't be as bad as usual. I filled a glass with water and sat down at my place.

"Could you get everyone else something to drink, Tatum?" Belén looked at me with disdain from the stove, like I should have known to serve everyone. Oops.

I pursed my lips, stood, and filled three more water glasses. As I set them down, Blanche winked at me. I gave her a small smile.

Once everyone was seated and Belén had said the blessing, which she did every night without fail, I filled my bowl to the brim and started shoveling it in. Apparently, manual labor made me really, really hungry. The clanging of silverware and porcelain ceased, and I looked up.

"What?" I said, which came out garbled because of the spoonfuls of happiness crowding my mouth. Belén and Tilly were looking at me like I was born in a barn, and Blanche was trying not to snicker.

"Why don't you tell us about your first day at work, Tatum?" Blanche's eyes crinkled in the corners, and I brightened.

"It's community service, Abuela," Tilly pointed out.

"Hush, Matilda. Let's let Tatum speak for herself. So?"

I swallowed and focused on Blanche. "It was okay. A lot of hard work. You have to use regular garden tools to clip branches, which can be super tedious. But it wasn't terrible. There are a couple of kids I know from school doing it too."

Blanche smiled warmly. "It's always better to do difficult tasks with friends."

Belén frowned. "I hope you're actually working and not socializing the whole time. Don't forget you have to get your supervisor to sign off on your hours, and if you're talking instead of working, I highly doubt you will earn his or her signature. You're not there to make friends, Tatum; you're there to do penance."

Penance? Was this the Middle Ages? "I know. My supervisor—her name is Alicia—put us in pairs. We work with the buddy system."

"You just make sure you obey all of Alicia's rules." Belén took a birdlike bite of soup and chewed for what felt like an hour. "Have you spoken to the Schmidts? Do you have a schedule worked out? I need to put it on the calendar."

Belén, in addition to color-coded spare keys, had a color-coded and meticulously labeled calendar that had all of the family activities and appointments on it. I couldn't deny it was helpful, since one of us was almost always somewhere doing something, but seeing my every move recorded for everyone to observe was a little disconcerting, a little Big Brother. It also made me sad to see "Ken—Out of Country" written on so many days.

I looked her straight in the eye and lied. It felt like the only way to get away from the new, stricter regime of our house and get a little time to myself. "I'll be watching the girls evenings only, so it won't conflict with the park service."

"Perfect. And just so you're aware, I will be writing

down the mileage on your car when you leave for their house and when you return, so don't even think about going somewhere else."

My jaw popped open when she dropped that bomb. "Was that your idea, or did you read it on your favorite blog?"

She shook her head and set her fork down. "You have to learn responsibility. Someone has to make you accountable." I hated how she automatically assumed the most restrictive method was the best.

Turns out I was wrong about dinner being tolerable. Not even Blanche or delicious food could change my stepmother.

"I'm not hungry anymore," I said between gritted teeth.

With my heart pounding in my chest and my legs shaking, I pushed out from the table and stomped up the stairs to my room, and slammed the door as hard as I could, rattling the pictures on my walls. I slid down to the floor and squeezed my eyes shut so tight that I started seeing little spots of light behind my lids. I exhaled and opened them. I had a sudden urge to call my dad, even though I knew he was asleep halfway across the world, and tell him what Belén was doing to me, but I didn't think it was going to do any good. What if this new development had been his idea?

I decided to write to him instead.

Hi Dad,

Just wanted to say hello. My first day removing plants is in the books, and it went pretty well. Some kids from school are working there too, so at least

I'm not alone, and my partner and I got a lot of nasty stuff cleared. In other news, it's hot. How hot is it there?

Love, Tatum

I pressed send. Ten seconds later, my email dinged. Had Dad responded already? Nope. But someone had sent the very first email to my new TLC inbox!

To Whom It May Concern,

I picked up your card at the McIntosh High School Summer Showcase last week and I was happy to see that you offer design services. I am a rising senior at MHS, and was interested in having you create a book cover for the science fiction novel I plan on self-publishing. I have some general thoughts on what it should include, but I'm curious what someone with design experience would have to suggest. Please respond as soon as you can.

Thanks for your time,
Emily Berger

It had been sent from a McIntosh.edu address. A little thrill started in my chest and rose to my throat, where it exited my body in a yelp. My first official client! Not that Abby wasn't official, but I already knew her, and I didn't have my own business when she asked me to do her site.

I jumped up out of the chair and did a little dance, not unlike those I'd seen football players do in the end zone. This was my end zone. A bright spot in an otherwise pathetically awful night. Someone, this Emily Berger, whoever she was, was willing to take a chance on me. She was putting her publishing dreams in my hands. She was asking me to make her look good. Something shimmered in my veins; it felt a little like joy, though that emotion was relatively foreign as of late. I allowed myself a small smile and sat back down to write back to Emily.

> Dear Emily,
>
> Thank you so much for reaching out. I would be glad to put something together for you. If you could please fill out the attached questionnaire and include your thoughts on the cover, I'll write up a proposal, which you can look over and let me know what you think, as well as make changes or suggestions. If you're interested in seeing some of my previous work, please visit the link below. If you'd like to speak to a current client about her experience, Abigail Gold's contact information is also below. I look forward to hearing from you and hopefully working with you soon.
>
> Sincerely,
> TLC

Was *Sincerely* the best way to close? I was starting to think I had a valediction complex, I was worrying about it so much. I wanted to come across as professional, but also approachable and fun. I thought for a second, held back from googling the list again, and changed *Sincerely* to:

> Cheers,
> TLC

I was careful to stick with my faux alias, just in case this somehow made it back to Tilly. She could be friends with this Emily person, for all I knew. I typed in the URL for my website, which was still a work in progress, and added Abby's email address under "References" at the bottom of the email. I didn't think Abby'd mind, especially since this whole thing was her idea. I also attached my brand-spanking-new client preferences survey for Emily to fill out so I could start brainstorming. My index finger hovered over the keyboard. I wished I had my keychain to rub for luck, but without it I crossed my fingers instead and sent my reply out into the ether.

I leaned back in my chair, possible cover ideas whizzing around my head faster than Katniss's arrows. Just for grins, I pulled up Photoshop and fiddled around. After a while, the door to my room edged open. The smell of something warm and spicy hit me before I saw Blanche set a full bowl down next to me. She bent over my shoulder and looked at the screen.

"New project?"

"New client," I whispered.

Blanche squeezed my shoulder lightly. "Am I allowed to say I told you so?"

I laughed. "I guess so."

"So just one new client so far?" She leaned up against the desk, facing me.

"Just one. But I gave a bunch of business cards and pens to the PTA lady at the thingy last weekend. She actually looked a little impressed."

"Good girl," Blanche said softly. "I know it hasn't

been easy for you, Tatum. I think creating things will be good for you."

My breath caught, and I struggled to respond. Her kindness was going to undo me. "I think so too."

Blanche patted me on the shoulder again and left me alone in the room, my thoughts still churning like the spin cycle, but no longer about Emily's book cover.

"Hey there, Mr. Blue." I tapped on the glass of the fish tank. The brilliantly blue beta, named only as a preschooler could, swam lazily toward me, and even though his little fishy expression stayed the same, I imagined he was staring at me with disinterest.

"Cheeky little guy," I said with a laugh. It wasn't until I dropped some food flakes into the top of his bowl that he moved with purpose. "That's right. Eat up, buddy." I replaced the cap and put the food container back on Kate's dresser.

I exited her fairy-themed bedroom—decorated in pink, pink, and more pink—and moved next door to Maya's slightly more subdued blue-and-green animal sanctuary. The hamster, Princess Sweetheart, was asleep in her little plastic cave, so I quickly replaced her food pellets and changed the water. She never stirred. "Sweet dreams, Your Highness," I whispered, and headed downstairs to fill Gus's bowl.

When I'd left the house, Belén had checked the mileage on my odometer as promised. She entered the

Schmidts' address into her phone's map app and told me I should add no more than six point four miles to the number on the dash.

"If you go anywhere other than their house, Tatum, there will be consequences." She stared at me, using her full height, practically singeing my eyebrows with her judgment lasers.

"There and back," I said, and saluted her. At least that part of the lie was true. As I'd turned to go, I caught a glimpse of her face wearing an unmistakable look of sadness. What was that about? Surely she couldn't be feeling guilty about playing bad cop. I wanted to ask her, but by the time I opened my mouth, she did an about-face and clacked back into the house.

I was actually looking forward to the peace and quiet of the Schmidt house, just me and the animals. The worst they could do was scratch me. My house was quiet—sometimes it was like a tomb even when all four of us were there. Silent and also a little creepy. But this was different. Away from home, I could get actual solitude. A time to relax. Rejuvenate.

Animals fed and watered, I sat down on the cushy couch in the living room, sinking into the overstuffed pillows as Gus lounged at my side. Kate and Maya loved to make forts out of those pillows, draping them with sheets from their bedrooms and crouching on hands and knees underneath, pretending they were spelunking in a treacherous cave or deep-sea diving for pearls. They always made sure to turn on their play camping lantern, just the right size for adventuring in the safety of their own home.

I missed them. It would have been fun to hang out with those ridiculous little girls this summer. Instead, their introverted pets would have to do.

I'd brought my laptop with me, hoping to get some work done on Emily's book cover proposal without the worry of Belén or Tilly walking in and asking what I was doing. A little voice in my head was saying I should have told them the truth about pet sitting. There wasn't really any particular reason to not tell them, since it wasn't like I was doing anything wrong, but I didn't want Belén to shut me down and keep me in the house any more than she already did. Now didn't seem to be the right time to bring it up with her. Maybe later . . . when she wasn't quite so mad at me over the whole "getting arrested" debacle.

Emily had sent me a vague idea for her cover—gears—and she'd also sent back the questionnaire, meant to help me figure out the best representative colors and style. Besides loving the obvious *Doctor Who* and *Firefly*, like all card-carrying sci-fi fans, she also liked Hitchcock movies and *CSI,* in all varieties and iterations. Emily was a mystery junkie. My gut told me starting with something in black and white might be a good plan.

I emailed her back.

> Dear Emily,
>
> This is really helpful, thank you so much. Could you send me a couple sample chapters or a synopsis of the book so I can make sure my idea will work?
>
> Cheers,
> TLC

I sent it off and snuggled deeper into the pillows. I closed my eyes and started having visions of Emily's book winning awards, and all the fanfare my spectacular cover might garner in the process. This business could very well be a springboard to something bigger for me. College. A job. Self-actualization. The possibilities were endless. Maybe.

My email dinged, and I struggled to sit up in the midst of the mountain of down and canvas. I had to use both hands to push myself out of the crevice. Best darn couch ever.

> Dear TLC Design,
>
> I'm interested in putting together an online portfolio for college. Is that something you can help me with? Please let me know.
>
> Thanks,
> SK

Another client! And, it was another McIntosh email address. God bless Blanche and her evil-genius mind. SKipsang@McIntosh.edu, it said. Why did I know that name? I was sure I'd heard it somewhere. I replied immediately. No point in wasting time where there was fine money to earn.

> Hi SK,
>
> Yes, I can definitely help you. Please see the link below for examples of my work. What kind of portfolio do you need?
>
> Cheers,
> TLC

I typed my website at the bottom and pressed send. I sat on the edge of the couch, not wanting to fall back into the black hole, in case my new potential client was still online and wrote back right away. Thirty seconds later, another ding. Assumption correct.

> Thanks for getting back to me so fast. I play cello. I'd like it to have my musical résumé and some audio files, at the bare minimum.
>
> SK

Cello! This was the musician whose performance poster I'd bashed at the McIntosh showcase. Oops. At least he hadn't designed it. Remembering looking at that poster, I blushed. I'd been critiquing it next to an amazingly gorgeous and intelligent guy. My fist smacked into the fluffy couch. I was still mad at myself for not asking him what his name was. Maybe SK or Emily knew him. Maybe I could ask them. Or maybe not. Because emailing a perfect stranger and saying "Hi, do you know an incredibly attractive guy with brown skin, dark hair, and sea-green eyes? Can you tell him I've been drooling over him? Okay, thanks so much" wouldn't be the least bit disturbing. Strike that idea.

> SK,
>
> That's easy to take care of. If you fill out the attached survey, I will start putting together a proposal for you ASAP.
>
> Cheers,
> TLC

I was very much enjoying using "cheers." It made me feel like I was from somewhere far away, like England or Scotland. Continuing my earlier fantasy, I started thinking about when it would be my turn to apply to college and leave the house. Belén had already started dropping hints about standardized testing. I could move way up north and totally reinvent myself. Get a fresh start and not have to live in the shadow of my perfect stepsister and a false accusation. Just as I was picturing myself walking across a campus dotted with red- and yellow-leaved trees, wooly scarf around my neck and latte in my hand, my email dinged again.

Question: Are you British by any chance? The "cheers" made me curious.
I'll fill out the survey this week. Thanks.
SK

Apparently, my new favorite valediction was a good conversation starter. This SK person didn't know who I was; maybe this was a good chance to try out my clean-slated self. Was clean-slate Tatum someone who answered emails five seconds after receiving them, like an eager beaver? Probably not—she'd play it cool, hold back more. I sank back into the couch of comfort, scratched Gus behind the ears, and clicked on the enormous flat-screen television. The Schmidts had every cable channel known to man, which was a little overwhelming. Belén thought TV was a waste of time if it wasn't the news, so we had a very basic package. Her TV watching came in two speeds; she was either silent and focused, concentrating so much it made my eyes hurt, or very loud, encouraging the presenters to get a new job. In fact, that was pretty much the way she approached everything in life. Me included.

I flipped through the channels, amazed at the sheer variety of options; most of the shows I knew only from the celebrity magazines Ash and I loved. Getting to actually watch them felt like a commandeered luxury. I settled on a cooking show where home chefs went from kitchen failures to seasoned—pun intended—experts. I'd never been much of a cook, but in the spirit of clean-slate Tatum, I felt inspired to pay attention. Maybe I would learn something new, just like the contestants. I rested my head on the back of the couch and put my feet up on the coffee table. The silver of my sandals winked at me in the TV's reflection. After a little relaxing, the antsiness came back, and I checked my watch. Ten minutes had passed. Clean-slate Tatum could respond to the email now, yes? Yes.

I hovered my hands over the laptop and tried to think of a witty response.

Hi SK,

Unfortunately not, but I play someone British on TV. From your reaction, it appears all that money I spent on acting lessons was worth it. I'll have to give my coach a raise. Okay, no, not really. I just like cheers as a professional-but-friendly valediction. Are YOU British?

CHEERS,
TLC

Maybe it wasn't actually witty, more like psychotic rambling, but it would have to do. And what if he did actually turn out to be British? Accents were cool. I went back to my cooking show, where the contestants were pulling soufflés, at varying degrees of sunk and burnt, out of the ovens. Despite the dubious appearances, my stomach rumbled at the sight of the fancy entrées. Gus eyed me suspiciously at the noise, and then went back to ignoring me.

Ding!

> TLC (Do you have an actual name btw?)—I myself am not British. I am half-Irish, though, and actually Irish, since my mom is ROB.

He left off the SK that time. This was getting awfully casual and familiar. Definitely not so professional. Did he assume I was his age? I mean, for all he knew, I could be a middle-aged guy who still lived with his mother.

> I do have a name, yes—had it since I was born, actually. I'm pro-Ireland. Your mom's name is Rob?

I laughed at my response, despite myself. This felt like a game. His answer came in about ten seconds. I wondered if he thought this was fun too.

> Wise guy. You're really going to make me work for it, aren't you? My mom's name is actually Eileen. ROB=right off the boat, aka recent immigrant. Also potentially offensive, but my mother uses that phrase about herself (even though she's been here twenty years), so I tend to forget it might annoy

someone else. You seem like a girl with a sense of humor, though.

I started typing a response as soon as I finished reading. Farewell, clean-slate Tatum and her amazing restraint. I liked this kid.

> What makes you think I'm female? And no worries, I'm not offended. Cool about your mom. Does she have a super-awesome accent? Do you have a pet leprechaun?

I was curious how much he thought he knew about me. Paranoid, I checked the webcam on my laptop. Still off, phew.

> Ah, caught. Mrs. Porter, who was manning the info booth at school the other night, handed me your business card and told me a cute girl was looking for clients. As I needed help with the portfolio and I am generally a fan of cute girls, I figured it was win-win for me. I do realize that the cute girl might have been the errand runner for someone else, so if you are in fact male or not a high school student, I truly apologize for the misstep. Which begs the question—are you?

Here was the moment of truth. Did I tell him he was right about me, or keep the mystery up? I supposed it didn't do any harm to share a little bit about myself. Building rapport was something Belén was forever chastising me for not doing enough, so here was a good opportunity for me to practice.

Guilty. I delivered the swag myself. My first attempt at finding clients, actually. I started this business at the insistence of a friend whose logo I designed. Seemed like a good use of my time and talent. I hope so, at least. Thanks for taking a chance on a newb.

You didn't answer my question about the leprechaun. Inquiring minds are dying to know.

Was he flirting? It felt like flirting, but I could never tell with the Internet. So much potential for miscommunication. Was I flirting back?

Ding!

My leprechaun actually got deported. He brought illegal "items" into the country when he arrived, and DHS sent him right back. Such a shame. I think about him every time I see a rainbow.

Your work is great, btw. Did you ever apply to McIntosh? Our art department could've used you.

Dagger. Right in the heart. I flopped backward into the cushions so hard, my neck snapped forward a bit. Why was it that total strangers could see what the admissions department hadn't? At least I had plenty of time to make a portfolio so amazing, no college could turn me down. Darn that wishful thinking again.

Sorry about your pet. Maybe a dog is a better option.

Thanks. I did apply two years ago, but alas, it wasn't meant to be.

It's Tate, btw. Nice to meet you.

I don't know what possessed me to use Tate instead of Tatum. Probably my subconscious playing a sick joke on me and reminding me that my best friend was still in ghost mode. My happy mood started to dissipate as quickly as it had shown up when I thought about that unanswered email I'd sent to Ash days ago. It bothered me so much that something as insignificant as an email conversation with a new client could remind me of my life's disappointments. But really, why should I be surprised? There were so many of them, after all. Belén's attitude toward me, Tilly's disinterest, the rejection from McIntosh. And somehow, losing Ash for something I thought was rather heroic hurt most of all. Brow furrowed and fists clenched, I closed the laptop. I couldn't look at praise from a perfect stranger anymore.

I checked my watch again; it was probably time to go home. If I was going to keep up this babysitting charade, I needed to make sure I got the timing correct. And Belén would know. I swear that woman had ESP or tracking devices in my shoes or something. She knew everything about everything. I gave Gus a goodbye cuddle and high-tailed it out of there.

When I pulled in at home, the door opened, and my beautifully awful stepmother came sauntering out the front door. She stuck her glossy black head in through my open window, noted the mileage, nodded with a "Thank you, Tatum," and disappeared back into the house. Well, then.

I grabbed my bags, put the window up, and turned off the ignition. It was going to be a long summer.

Chapter 7

"*T*atum!" Belén was standing at the bottom of the stairs, shouting my name like a banshee.

"Seriously, Stepmother?" I said to myself, rolling over. I looked at the clock on my nightstand. It was 5:37 a.m. The sun wasn't even up yet, and my room was still cozily dark. I rubbed my eyes and sat up, confused.

"Tatum! Your father's on the phone. Pick up." Her scream was even louder this time, which seemed impossible, but she did have an impressive set of lungs. She missed her calling as a football coach or something. I fumbled for the light, pulled back the covers, and shuffled over to my desk, where the landline sat.

"Hi, Dad." My voice was rough and craggy from sleep.

"Good morning, sweetheart. Did I wake you?" Dad sounded rather chipper. I guessed that meant his work was going well. He'd always had a bit of a Superman complex.

Dad liked finding solutions to problems; it made him happy.

"No, Belén's bellowing did."

Belén, still on the line, piped up. "It was time for you to get up anyway, Tatum."

I clenched my jaw. "Do you think I could talk to my dad alone for a minute? Please?" I added the *please* more for Dad's sake than Belén's.

A pause. What was there for her to think about? I tightened my clench, waiting for her to answer me.

"Certainly." The line clicked, and now there was just silence between me and Dad.

He made the first move. "How is the plant removal going? Sounds like you got a lot of work done that first day. Sorry I didn't get a chance to write you back, by the way, and for calling so early. I've been swamped."

"It's fine. I know you're busy. The stuff we're doing is really time consuming, but I think we're making a difference."

"That's great. A silver lining, eh?"

That might be pushing it. My entire summer probably wouldn't be turned around by the fact that removing invasive plants would make the environment safer, even though, weirdly, I was kind of happy to help. It would take something much bigger, more personal, to actually turn the summer around. Like regaining my family's trust.

"I think I'm making a difference here too," he went on, "so good for both of us."

"Yeah. Definitely." I was glad my dad was helping others—I was proud of the work he did—but a big part of me wanted him back here. "And I've been playing around with Photoshop too. Teaching myself some new techniques."

Completely true. I wanted to tell him about how I might be starting a business. I just wasn't sure if this was my moment.

"That's wonderful, and I can't wait to see what you've come up with. Send me something you've been working on, okay?"

"Okay, sure." My heart fluttered. Dad was my favorite art critic.

"And Belén tells me you're taking care of Maya and Kate again? That's great. I know Mrs. Schmidt appreciates the extra set of hands."

This time, my heart stopped cold. I felt horrible lying to my dad. He and I had always been honest with each other, but I was still angry with him. I was frustrated that he hadn't had more faith in me. I also wasn't willing to topple the house of cards I'd built for myself yet, which meant losing access to an actual, Belén-free home. Realistically, I knew there was always a chance the truth would come out in the end, but I was feeling just reckless enough to not be concerned about that yet.

"Yep. And their cat, hamster, and beta fish too." At least that part was true.

"That's nice." So predictable; I knew my dad wouldn't ask why the girls weren't taking care of their own pets. He had not been born with Belén's spidey senses.

"Speaking of which, did you know that Belén is recording the mileage on my car when I leave the house?"

Dad cleared his throat uncomfortably. "She's just trying to help you be accountable, Tatum." There was that word again. I was used to him just going with whatever Belén thought was best when it came to making the rules, but it had never been something this outrageous, and he usually saw my side of things after we talked. Did he approve of this new tactic, or was he simply too far away to fight for me?

"So she needs to control everything? I think there are better ways of teaching that concept, Dad." Even though he couldn't see me, I went ahead and made bunny ears when I said "teaching." "A sticker reward chart, perhaps? That worked when we were little." I got a sticker for making my bed and setting the table; Tilly got one for memorizing routines and sonatas. When he didn't respond right away, I knew I'd gone over the edge. "I just don't think it's fair, Dad," I said softly.

"Tatum, I know this is hard for you. It's hard for us too." He had on his quiet voice, confirming he'd had enough of my sass. I bit my lip to keep from saying anything more. "Just humor her. Do as she says, and by the end of the summer, it will be water under the bridge."

Some days I agreed with him and thought keeping my head down was easy; some days it felt like I was Sisyphus, rolling that huge rock up the hill, waiting for it to come down and flatten me.

I inhaled, and let the air out loudly. "I'll try."

"I love you, sweetheart. It's going to be okay."

My lower lip started trembling, and I bit it again; so hard, it hurt. "I know," I whispered. But I didn't. How could it be when he wasn't here?

Just when I thought the weather couldn't get any hotter, it got hotter. It shouldn't have surprised me, having lived in northern Virginia for the entire sixteen years of my life, but somehow the oppressive heat and drenching humidity always seemed like a cruel joke without a punch line. Clipping the sickly sweet honeysuckle branches in the fully overhead noontime sun wasn't fun anymore, not that it really was to begin with.

Abby came dressed to work, and by dressed, I mean completely covered. The second week of our "internship," she'd abandoned her athletic tank top in favor of a long-sleeved Jimi Hendrix T-shirt. Hunter had worn a Jimi shirt on the third day. Abby had an abundance of chutzpah, which was part of why I liked her, though it probably would have been easier if she just bit the bullet and talked to Hunter, instead of risking the heatstroke she was guaranteed to get.

"You're not being obvious or anything," I said as we slipped on our gloves. I had slathered on the high-octane sunscreen before leaving the house, and my skin stuck to the canvas fabric.

Abby pouted and lowered her head slightly, causing her dark brown curls to graze her shoulders. "I was going for conversation starter. Too much?"

I nodded my head. "Of course not." She smacked me in the arm with her gloves.

"Smart aleck."

"Always."

She slipped the gloves on and picked up her garden shears—long, dangerous scissors that looked more like some kind of illegal weapon than a useful tool—and started walking toward what we'd affectionately started calling "our" honeysuckle. We'd made more progress on it the last few sessions, but it was still gigantic.

Abby pointed her shears in the direction of Hunter and his asthmatic partner's section, still covered with ivy. "Neither one of them is here today?"

I glanced over at the empty area. "Guess not? Maybe the kid is at home blowing his nose. Maybe Hunter got a clue and decided shredding ivy wasn't as fun as he thought it was going to be."

"Maybe," she said sadly. "By the way, I got my site up and running. Posted a movie review this morning, in fact."

"That's amazing, congrats. Did you get your business cards printed?"

"Yes, they're ordered. I used your referral code, so you'll get a discount on your next order."

"If I ever have to order again. I've gotten a few bites, but nothing new this week." And nothing new from SK. Not that it bothered me. Nope. He hadn't sent back the survey yet, though, so the proposal for his portfolio site was at a standstill.

"What kinds of requests are you getting?" Abby snagged a long, twisty vine and wrestled it to the ground with both her hands and feet like it was an alligator in a swamp.

"The two so far—besides you, of course—are both McIntosh students, seniors."

"Of course," she said, and rolled her eyes. I'd learned Abby was bitter that McIntosh didn't have a journalism program.

"One's a writer. She has a book she wants me to design a cover for. It's steampunk."

Abby pumped a fist into the air. "Love it."

"Really? I have no idea what that is, other than that she wants something with gears." Abby nodded, like this made total sense. I'd definitely have to do some more research on the genre.

"I'll educate you, give you some covers to take a look at. And the other?"

"This guy who plays the cello, named SK. He wants me to make an online portfolio about his musical career to submit to colleges with his applications."

After a beat, I realized the rustling of branches had ceased, and I looked up. Abby was staring at me.

"Do I have dirt on my face or something?" I wiped my gloves on my backside and brought my fingertips to my cheeks, prepared to wipe.

She shook her head. "No dirt. But tell me more about SK."

I must have started blushing, or the sun moved, because my cheeks got hotter. "Why do you ask?"

"When you said his name, you smiled. That doesn't happen very often."

"What? Me smiling?" I automatically frowned. I smiled plenty, didn't I? And then I remembered how Blanche thought I was melancholy. Maybe I didn't.

"Yeah. So naturally, being a reporter, I need more

information. What's the deal?" Abby pantomimed flicking open her invisible notebook, invisible pen poised to take notes.

I pressed my mouth into a firm line and turned back to my vines. "Nothing. I think. We exchanged a few emails that were kind of flirty, but maybe I'm just lonely and misinterpreting. It's not like we even know each other. It was three or four emails. And it doesn't matter anyway, because he hasn't even sent the info I need to work on his portfolio, so I think it's a moot point. For all I know, he was just feeling it out and decided I was a loser, and isn't going to actually hire me." The words tumbled from my mouth like stones dropping into a well, splashing with self-doubt as I spoke.

Abby put her shears down on the ground, took off her gloves, tossed them into the dirt, and grabbed the sleeve of my gray Georgetown T-shirt. She pulled me toward her until I was near enough for her to wrap her skinny, freckled arms around my shoulders. She squeezed gently.

"What was that for?" Her gesture stunned me. There wasn't much hugging in my life with Dad gone.

She shrugged. "Sounded like you needed it."

The corners of my mouth lifted ever so slightly. "Thanks. These haven't exactly been the best few weeks of my life, to tell you the truth."

She nodded and picked her shears back up. "I know." She tapped her head. "Reporter, remember? I pay attention."

I nodded back at her once and turned back to my vines. Maybe Abby wasn't the only one being obvious.

Just like her outfit was a beacon for Hunter, signaling him to profess his undying devotion to her, my sudden, odd, and probably inappropriate attachment to a potential client, whose only "conversation" had been a handful of jokes made over the interwebz, was a blinking neon sign that I was in need of some kind of intervention. Or maybe just a friend. My fingers twitched slightly, my hand eager to slip into my pocket and make contact with my keys, and I chastised myself for forgetting that what I wanted wasn't there anymore.

Settling in on the Schmidts' couch, I opened my laptop, intending to finish up Emily's cover proposal. To my shock and amazement, a small bomb exploded in my inbox instead.

> Hi Tate,
>
> Sorry I took forever to get back to you. No rest for the weary when it comes to music unfortunately. I shouldn't complain; I love it. But a man needs a break sometimes. Also, your survey is wicked hard. I hope my answers are helpful, but some questions made me feel like I was filling out an online dating profile. What do you do with them anyway?
>
> SK

I opened the attachment he'd sent with his email with a smirk on my face. My questions were thought-provoking, but I certainly wouldn't have called them "wicked hard." Did he not self-reflect? Was I the only one who did that? I shrugged to myself and read on.

Name: Seamus Kipsang

DOB: February 19

Location: Vienna, VA

Occupation: cellist and student (does this count as an occupation? No one is paying me . . . yet)

Favorite Color: Brown

Brown? Who liked brown? This is the question that probably gets asked more in a lifetime than anything else, and he picked brown? That made me a little nervous for his mental state and his judgment.

Favorite Music: This is the worst question for me to answer, by the way. You can't ask a musician to pick a favorite. I have a list. I love Bach and Beethoven, but who doesn't? My current favorite modern classical musician is Tanya Anisimova. She's from Russia but lives in Virginia now. She taught a master class at school last year, and I fell in love. I'm hoping to play something of hers for my senior recital next year. Does that make me sound like a geek? Probably. Non-classical, I really love Ben Howard, Halsey, The Lumineers, Hozier, Neko Case, Ben Folds, Mumford and Sons, Sarah Jarosz . . . I could keep going if you need more.

I immediately googled Anisimova and found a gorgeous cello and harp duet on YouTube. I'd never been much of a classical music fan, probably from lack of exposure other than whatever Tilly was practicing on the piano, but the notes she played and the way she dragged the bow methodically across her instrument slayed me. The musical honey seeped over me; my chest tightened and my breath caught in my throat as I listened. I had to turn it off so I wouldn't cry. The cello struck me as such a sad instrument, wallowing in grief or overcome with turmoil, but maybe that was just my state of mind projecting.

> Favorite TV Show: Not much of a TV watcher, but I
> do follow sports. I might have a slight obsession
> with the All Blacks.

Hmm, no idea what that meant.

> Favorite Movie: Any old school horror movie.
> Especially *The Shining* and *Carrie.*

Carrie happened to be my most favorite movie of all time. Something about her isolation and loneliness had always struck me. Not to mention the wacky mom. Go figure.

> Hobbies: I wish I had more to write here, but I've
> pretty much already answered it above. I play
> music, I watch rugby, I lift weights, and I hang out
> with my family. That's basically it. There isn't a lot
> of time for anything else, though I'm hoping that'll
> change in college.

Aside from the hanging out with family, which I only did when forced, and the watching rugby—because why would I spend my time watching sweaty guys run into each other?—and replace the music with design, we were just alike. I chuckled. Right. I knew I was grasping at straws for some kind of connection. A connection that was only in my mind. Clearly.

> Personal Style: Like clothes? I'm a jeans and T-shirts guy. Is that relevant?

I frowned. That one bordered on dating website for sure. I'd used it because it could be useful in coming up with a style for a site or a logo. I didn't want to use primary colors and Comic Sans—shudder—for someone who wore suits and shiny dress shoes every day. Maybe I should've taken that question out.

> Pizza Toppings: WHY DO YOU NEED TO KNOW THIS? DO YOU SEND YOUR CLIENTS PIZZA? Now I'm hungry, of course. I like pepperoni and mushrooms. I have this thing about too many toppings. It hides the taste of the crust and the cheese and it makes the slice all floppy, and there is absolutely nothing worse than floppy pizza. Am I right?

I squeezed my eyes shut so the tears wouldn't come streaming out. Tears of laughter this time, though. I started reading that answer and began laughing immediately; my lungs ached and my sides burned by the time I could control myself again.

I had a very valid reason for asking that question. A pretty sneaky one, if I did say so myself. And SK's answer proved my theory perfectly. There are always exceptions, but in my experience, people who liked plain cheese or just one topping were often minimalists. I couldn't very well give that client a site or a poster loaded with icons and words and patterns and blinking lights, now could I? These people were Ikea. Clean lines, a singular color, simple fonts, less is more, words that made an impact. People who liked "the works" on pizza liked things everywhere. I imagined that people who ordered every topping on the menu also had piles of magazines and newspapers in their homes, ten knickknacks on every shelf, and a bow tied on anything that would stand still. For those clients, I might use the full spectrum of colors, various fonts, a slideshow of photographs, all the bells and whistles. In other words, the pizza-topping question was a litmus test.

I wiped my eyes and read the final answer.

> Any other relevant preferences: Now that I'm at the end, I am literally dying to know what you're going to use these answers for. Please, if you have any compassion, divulge your secrets, O Wise One. I don't have anything else to add, other than I'm a little scared of you now.

I giggled and started typing back a response.

> SK,
>
> Sorry if I stumped you. Don't you need to know your answers to these types of questions for college apps? You should probably get used to this kind of interrogation. Your answers help me figure out what kind of person you are so I can decide

what kind of design would best represent you. You actually answered the pizza topping question perfectly. Very helpful.

What's an All Black?

Carrie is my favorite movie too. Small world.

So, based on your answers, I'm going to make a simple site without a lot of fluff, but that is a little whimsical, and highlights your musical career. Yes?

Tate

P.S.—Can you please send me a detailed résumé?

P.P.S.—Brown???

I pressed *send* and stretched out on the couch, where I promptly fell asleep. What felt like minutes later, the music on the television—the theme song to some wacky reality show about a little girl wearing way too much makeup—woke me with a jolt. I checked the clock on the cable box and saw it was well past the time Belén would be expecting me home. I groaned loudly, snatched up my bag and laptop, and sped back home.

Belén was waiting for me at the door when I pulled in. "Why are you late, Tatum?" She tapped her toe, still clad in the pumps she'd left the house in that morning, on the hardwood floor of the entryway. Her signature move.

Sometimes I wondered what it was like being inside her head. I imagined it was like a pinball game, with thoughts and opinions zooming around and slamming into her skull, setting off bells and alarms. I had to take a deep breath just thinking about that kind of chaos.

I squared my shoulders, hoping to pull off a please-believe-me stance. "Well, Belén," I said calmly, "as it turns out, the Schmidts had some car trouble on the way home. They said to apologize for any trouble they've caused you." The lie rolled off my tongue a little too easily.

She raised an eyebrow, and I raised one right back. Before she could say anything to contradict me, I marched forward in a fashion that mimicked what I saw daily from her and went into the house. I might have made a victory face as well, but I definitely did not turn around for her to see.

Tilly, ruled by early dance practices and her mother's iron-fisted grip, had probably gone to bed long ago. In moments of fleeting compassion for her, I felt bad that she had such a rigid schedule. That was always quickly swatted away, since I knew dancing was a choice she'd made. The soft glow of the television illuminating the basement stairs told me that Blanche was still awake. I practically tripped down the stairs, not interested in spending more time with only myself for company in the silence of my room. Blanche was on the couch, which wasn't nearly as lovely and smooshy as the one at the Schmidts' house, her perfectly tiny feet crossed on the coffee table.

I hovered in the doorway, hoping she'd invite me to join her.

Hearing my footsteps, Blanche looked up. Her brown eyes met mine, and she smiled. "Hello, Tatum. How was your evening?"

"Fine. Just did my job. How was yours?" I shifted my weight from one foot to the other, not wanting to talk about my job. At all.

She reached a hand into the pocket of her cropped pants and pulled out a fistful of five-dollar bills. "I won bunco!"

I laughed at the proud, jovial expression on her face. "What's bunco?"

"A dice game old women play for money." She smirked. "My friend Carolina is out of town for the summer; I think I mentioned this to you the other day. I'm taking her place in the weekly game while she's gone."

"And you won on your first shot?" I raised my eyebrows, impressed. But also, not surprised. It was Blanche, after all.

"It seems that way. A bit of luck, that's all." Blanche chuckled and put the bills back in her pocket. She patted the empty space to her left. I knew better than to hesitate.

"Better not let Belén see you with your feet on the table like that. She'll bust out the Pledge and make you polish it." I flopped down next to her and promptly put my feet up right beside hers, sandals still on.

"If she has a problem with feet on tables, she can wipe up the nonexistent marks herself." Blanche's eyes went back to the television screen. She was watching an episode of *The Golden Girls*. Anyone who liked funny TV and didn't need everything in her house to be just so was all right with me.

"Can I move in with you?" Living with Blanche, where I could be relaxed and not on guard twenty-four/seven sounded pretty great right about now.

"I think your father might miss you."

"No one else would."

"I don't know about that."

I disagreed, but bit my tongue. I'd never felt like I was anything more than an inconvenience for Belén. A fly she needed to keep swatting away. I could just see the sigh of relief she'd let out if I left for my stepgrandmother's house.

Blanche pointed to the screen. "You know what I love about this show? They argue and bicker, and yet they're still the best of friends. They're four totally different people, and somehow they find ways to love each other in spite of those differences."

I side-eyed her. "Are you trying to tell me something wise? Teach me a life lesson?" I hoped not. I didn't need one of the very few people who seemed to be in my corner crossing over to the dark side.

"Tatum, you are free to interpret my words any way you like. I was simply expressing what I like about a television show." She smiled, still watching the screen. "Did you know that this is how I improved my English?"

"Watching Dorothy and Sophia go head to head?"

She nodded. "Exactly. When we came to the United States from Chile over thirty years ago, I knew English, but not as well as I would have liked. One of our friends who had immigrated at the same time told me that watching American television programs would help, so that's what I did. *The Golden Girls* was my favorite."

A thought occurred to me. "Did you name yourself Blanche after that Blanche?" I stifled a giggle at the possibility of this diminutive, sweet-yet-sly woman renaming herself after a geriatric tart.

"Yes. I like her because she knows who she is and doesn't apologize for it." She looked over at me pointedly.

Suuure, this wasn't a teachable moment. Blanche had metaphor written all over her face.

"Yeah, yeah, yeah. Why can't it just be a TV show?" As much as I appreciated her and the sentiment, my brain was stuffed so full of this so-called life wisdom that it was starting to leak out my ears; there wasn't room for more.

"Why would it be anything else, Tatum?" She turned back to the show, put a hand on my knee, and squeezed gently.

Tate,

The All Blacks are only the very best rugby team in the world. How do you not know this? Look up a video of the Haka. It'll blow your mind. I've been trying to convince my orchestra friends to do it with me before a concert, at least once before we graduate.

Brown is the color of chocolate. And toasted marshmallows. Need I say more?

I think you nailed me. With that site, that is.

SK

P.S.—What's *your* favorite color?

Of course I couldn't not look up this mysterious Haka, which turned out to be a bunch of beefy New Zealand rugby players doing a kind of tribal war dance. It was both terrifying and mesmerizing.

SK,

That was wild. Kinda makes me want to see it in person.

Don't forget to send me your résumé!

I like green and silver.

Tate

I went to sleep that night with violently red cheeks, thoughts of chocolate, and the sounds of Maori chanting in my head.

Chapter 8

"Can I join your group? My partner bailed on me."
Hunter approached Abby and me as we were shaking
open the gigantic black garbage bags to start clipping,
once more, our beloved honeysuckle.

I was starting to get attached to our little area, having
become friendly with this plant we were destroying. I
felt bad for it. Even though Alicia repeatedly reminded us
that we were doing the right thing by removing it, that it
would be better for the rest of the noninvasive plants and
the native animals, I felt a twinge of guilt with every clip.
It smelled pretty. The flowers were sweet. Looks could be
deceiving, it seemed.

Abby blanched, in a moment lacking her usual bra-
vado. "Sure. I mean, did Alicia say it was okay?"

He shrugged. "Didn't ask. I figured as long as the
plants were getting the boot, she wouldn't care."

I handed him a bag. "What happened to the young Padawan?"

"My guess? He sneezed himself right out of here. That kid is allergic to everything. I was beginning to think it was contagious."

"Why the heck would he apply for a position like this?" Seemed like a no-brainer to me.

"Right? He told me he had been studying plants since he was little, which made me laugh since he's little now—seventh grade."

I laughed. "Guess he'd better stick with reading about them and not experiencing them."

Hunter and I bumped fists and Abby let out a loud cackle, totally out of character for her, and definitely not her normal laugh. I gave her the side eye.

"So true," she said, loudly, nodding her head so hard, her curls were flying back and forth.

As Hunter stepped to the side to shake open his plastic bag, I leaned in toward Abby. "What was that laugh? Back to obvious, are we?"

Abby just shrugged and smiled sweetly at me. With a sharp inhale, she sidled over to Hunter. "So what's going on with the band? Are you guys playing any gigs soon?"

"Yeah, we've been practicing, when we can, anyway. Some of the guys have other commitments; most are taking vacations at some point. The goal is to get it together enough to play at Sol Jam."

Abby clapped her hands. "That would be completely epic."

Epic? Abby was really laying it on thick. "What's Sol Jam?" I asked.

"End-of-summer concert. Been going on for years now. Outdoors, five or six local bands, lots of people. A friend of a friend's family has a place out toward The Plains with a gigantic field and no neighbors around to complain about the noise. Should be a good time. We played last year, and I'm hoping it works out again."

Abby watched him speak like he was a piece of talking chocolate cake. "Wow. That sounds amazing. Doesn't it sound amazing, Tatum?"

"Yes, amazing." If Hunter didn't know Abby was crushing on him, he was more clueless than she was. The romantic in me that threatened to come out every once in a while hoped it worked out for Abby. And Hunter too. Abby was a pretty great catch.

I grimaced. "It could use a better name, though. Sol Jam? Sounds like a thirteen-year-old named it."

Hunter shrugged sheepishly. "I think that's exactly who did name it. The guy who started it is in college now."

Suddenly, Abby smacked me in the arm. "I have the absolute best idea ever!"

I rubbed my forearm, brows knitted. "Better than finishing up this honeysuckle and moving to a new scary plant in the shade?" My jealousy of the pairs who had chosen spots away from the raging mid-July sun knew no bounds. It was boiling hot, and my nose kept prickling from the sweetness and the dust of the field.

"Yes." She turned to Hunter and put her hands up in front of her chest, gesturing wildly. "Hunter. Tatum just launched a graphic design business. You have an event that requires advertising. Tatum could make a poster for

Sol Jam. Her work is fabulous!" Abby had put on her "I
want to sell you something" voice that I knew she had to
use when convincing local businesses to buy ad space in
the school paper.

Hunter studied me for a moment, beads of sweat
forming at his hairline. "That could be cool." He moved
on to the last of the honeysuckle, and Abby and I followed. We clipped for a solid six or seven minutes before
he spoke again. "Do you have a card or something?"

"Yeah, in my car." I pointed back toward the parking lot.

"Cool," he repeated. "I'll check with my buddies.
Even if the property owner, Owen, doesn't want to
advertise, I'm sure making something up for just our band
and our fans would be okay." I was a little impressed that
Hunter's band had actual fans. "I'll let you know, okay?"

"Definitely."

Behind him, Abby squeeed silently. I rolled my eyes at
her and grinned. By the time we finished for the day, the
last of the honeysuckle had been packed tightly into the
plastic bags, all three of us had sweated through our shirts,
and I was still grinning.

While bringing the full bags to Alicia's flatbed truck
for disposal, Abby smacked me on the arm again. "I have
an even better idea!"

"Better?" I asked. "How is that possible? And why do
each of your ideas involve hitting me?" I smirked at her.

She ignored me and pressed on. "Hunter, what if
I were to do a whole spread on your band for the first
issue of the paper? I could, you know, come to practice,

interview the other members, take a bunch of photos. It'll be great." She turned to me. "Don't you think readers would like that, Tatum?" Abby's expression was pleading with me to support her.

"Oh right, yeah, for sure. I think that would be the most widely read issue in school history. Definitely," I deadpanned. Abby's blue eyes darkened in exasperation.

Hunter eyed us like girls were the weirdest creatures he'd ever seen. He took the bags from us and loaded them onto the flatbed with a *thunk*. "Maybe. I'd have to check with the band."

"It would be pretty amazing advertising," I said. Abby smiled at me gratefully. "For free, I might add."

"Exactly! This would be the best possible exposure. You end the summer with a bang and start the school year right." Abby nodded her head furiously, agreeing with herself.

I kept the ball rolling. "I bet you would get snapped up for sweet sixteens, quinceañeras, graduation parties. Maybe even the epitome of high school band achievements—a school dance."

Hunter looked at me in disbelief. I guessed his sarcasm detector was in the shop that day. "Like I said, I'll have to ask the guys. Not really something I can decide by myself, you know?"

"Of course, we understand," Abby said, "Make sure to mention that the deal includes the sparkling wit and intellect of two beautiful women." Two? Did she mean me? "That will definitely push them over the edge."

Hunter laughed at that, while I put a hand up in the

air to halt the conversation. "Pause please. Who is this 'we' you speak of?"

"You and me, silly. You're our resident designer. How else can you be expected to find inspiration without seeing your subjects close up? Hear the music?"

I shook my head. "Right, but you seem to forget that I'm not here"—I gestured to the park and the office building—"by choice. I am effectively under house arrest for the rest of the summer. There is no band practice for this girl." As much as I wanted to go to help Abby with her article and go to Sol Jam—which, despite the awkward name, sounded awesome—I couldn't go without Belén's approval. And there was no way she would let me out.

"The thing with Ashlyn?" Hunter questioned. I nodded slowly, my mouth suddenly dry. "I never heard exactly what happened." He looked at me expectantly, like it was no big deal to share personal details about my shady criminal past.

Abby's eyebrows lifted ever so slightly. I knew she'd been waiting for me to spill all the ugly details.

I gulped the humid air. No time like the present, and no use keeping it in any longer. "Right. So, there was this tiny misunderstanding at Mason's right before school ended."

Hunter and Abby stood still, like statues cemented to the insanely hot asphalt, as I told my tale of woe. They didn't move a muscle until I finished, closing my monologue with a scarily accurate impression of Belén reprimanding me for losing my keys. When I stopped speaking, I realized all the other kids had packed away their bags on the truck and left. The sound of Alicia turning on the engine jolted me back to the park and out of my nightmare, which was in fact still my reality. I looked down at the ground, shifted my weight, and tried to slow my heart rate, which had elevated as I spoke.

As the truck backed out and drove toward the main road, Hunter started shaking his head. "Dang, girl."

"Yep. That pretty much sums it up." I kicked a stray rock with my toe.

"How do you live with rules like that in your house? I'd go bananas." Hunter's face bore a look of disgust, which oddly annoyed me. It felt a little weird to hear someone besides me criticize Belén.

"Well, I guess . . ." I tried to be diplomatic. "She feels very . . . strongly that there's a right way to live your life."

"Don't all parents, though?" Abby asked.

"I guess so. I just wish her ideas weren't so . . ." I said, fumbling for the right word. "Narrow."

On some level, I got where Belén was coming from. She wanted Tilly and me to become productive citizens and go out into the world to do good things; I knew that at my core. I was just a little tired of defending why the things that made me happy were just as good as the ones she thought were best. I couldn't wait to be out on my own, where no one would be looking over my shoulder, evaluating everything like I was an employee or something.

Abby's sympathetic face was on, and she looked itchy to give me a hug, but also wary, like she was afraid that if she touched me, I might cry or break or punch her. Maybe all three.

"Do you hate her?" she asked in a small voice.

"Belén? No. She and I just don't see eye to eye."

"Ashlyn, I mean."

Oh. I pulled in a breath. "No, I don't hate her either."

As I said it, I knew it was the truth. We had too much shared history for me to ever *hate* her, no matter how upset or annoyed I was with my estranged best friend. The first day of middle school, when we were forced to "dress out" for gym for the first time, Ashlyn and I were randomly paired to share a locker. She was painfully thin, with blonde hair reaching the middle of her back, and had been doing her best to cover her chest, which was still too small for a bra but covered in one anyway. She slipped the gray cotton shirt over her head and shoulders as quickly as humanly possible. We'd eyed each other warily at first, making sure that our street clothes never touched as they rested side by side in the blue locker while we sat in lines, tween robots doing pushups and crunches at the sound of a whistle. When Mr. Barton, the PE teacher fresh out of college and still struggling to grow facial hair, made us do a timed mile run, Ashlyn and I discovered we both were terrible runners. We competed with each other for last place, and eventually we started to talk, and then to laugh. We vented about our lack of athletic skills, about our strict parents— Belén and her father—and about our absent parents—my dead mother and traveling father, and her mother, who spent her days at the spa and expensive lunches.

When Jeremy Wu dumped me in eighth grade after a lengthy three-week relationship (for a cheerleader with better calves than me), Ash invited me to sleep over at her house while we blacked his face out of every yearbook she owned. When Ashlyn was named second place in the regional geography bee, I was sitting in the audience cheering the loudest, glittery sign in hand. And also comforting her when her father chastised her for not knowing which body of water had the highest level of salinity. In addition to countless sleepovers, we'd eaten lunches together, studied at each other's homes, gone stag together to school dances. We'd both had other friends, of course—since she was far more obsessed with grades and test scores than I was, while I spent my free time in the computer lab or in the art room—but we always came back to each other, like boomerangs.

I wanted to believe that Ash would come back this time. We were bigger than this. Better than this. I just didn't know how long it would take her to get here.

Hunter was still shaking his head. "You're a better person than I am, Tatum. I would have walked and never looked back."

I flinched.

"Aren't you even mad? You seem kind of over it," Abby said.

"I'm definitely still mad. She made a choice that has pretty much ruined my life as I knew it. I'm holding out hope that she'll admit that to me one of these days. I'm mad that she decided to slum it with a complete moron who didn't have the brains to see the eight million holes in his grand plan to get rich quick. I'm mad that my dad all but ignored the fact that I was just trying to keep an eye on Ash, and that he left right when I needed him."

I was on a roll, why stop? "I'm mad that Ash's mistake

just confirmed I don't deserve my stepmother's time, attention, and, God forbid, affection. And because of Ash, the stepmonster felt I needed a babysitter every waking moment of the day, so she brought her mother—a very cool person, but still—to live with us for the whole summer. And I'm also mad that my perfect stepsister, who barely speaks to me as it is, can hardly look at me now."

We stood there quietly in the wake of the wave I'd just cast at them; no one dared speak. I looked down at my chest rising and falling, the cotton of my T-shirt sticking awkwardly to my skin. I pulled the sides of my shirt down over my hips and spoke in a voice half the size as before. "So to answer your question, yes, I'm mad. I think I'll probably be mad for quite a while."

This time, Abby didn't hesitate. She closed the distance between us and wrapped her arms, just as sweaty as mine, around me, our skin fusing together. I let her hold me, and closed my eyes as I rested my cheek on the mahogany curls lying on her shoulder. I heard Hunter's footsteps come behind me, and a hand patted the exposed space between my shoulder and Abby's arms.

"I'm just gonna go ahead and say yes to the newspaper story. We'd love to have you come see us play. Both of you."

I offered him a tentative smile. "I'd like that. I don't think I'll be able to make it happen. But I'm sure I'd like it."

Abby walked me to my car after we said goodbye to Hunter. "Hey, so, do you think your stepmother would let you come over to my house for dinner this week? We could talk about what we want to do for the article on the band. Maybe if she knows my parents will be there the whole time, she'll say yes?" Her face was so full of hope. I missed hope. I appreciated Abby's effort, and her concern for me, but I couldn't share her optimism.

"I will ask. My dad did say that all outings had to be approved ahead of time, but he didn't say outings were off limits."

Abby's eyes crinkled as she grinned. "All you can do is ask, right? Maybe she'll surprise you and say yes. Tell her she can even call my mom to confirm there'll be appropriate supervision." She winked when she said "appropriate."

I couldn't help laughing at her determination, but the little voice inside my head reminded me to not hold my breath.

When I came in the house, Belén was in the kitchen chopping cucumbers for a salad. I watched her make each cut with military precision, and wondered if she'd been watching my new favorite cooking show and learning about knife skills. No one else was around, so I knew this was my chance to ask her about going to Abby's. I inhaled, squared my shoulders, and set my keys down on the table with a clink. Belén looked up, startled.

"Tatum, you're home." It was more scientific observation than greeting. I knew I couldn't roll my eyes and have my request granted, so I forced a smile instead.

"Hi, Belén." She narrowed her eyes suspiciously. I

rarely called her by her name. "I wondered if you would allow me to have dinner with my friend, Abby Gold, and her family one night this week. Her parents have invited me to join them."

Belén's only reaction was to blink her long lashes. Well, then. How else could I convince her it was okay for me to go?

"I promise to call you when I get there and when I leave, and if you want to talk to Mrs. Gold for confirmation of my arrival, I'm sure she wouldn't mind."

Another blink.

"Please?"

Belén set down her knife, turned around, crossed her arms against her chest, and watched for a minute. My hands began to shake, so I knotted them behind my back and studied the chipped polish on my toenails to avoid her stare.

Finally, she spoke. "It's very generous of your friend's family to invite you, but I don't think it's a good idea."

My cheeks burned instantly. How could she say no? There was nothing deceitful about my request. Granted, she had never met Abby or her parents, but I'd offered a solution for that, hadn't I? I didn't understand.

"Why not?" I was practically whispering, the corners of my eyes stinging with almost-tears.

"I think you need to stay focused on your community service and your job. You don't need any distractions to steer you off course."

Were we on a ship now? I opened my mouth to retort and then realized what she wasn't saying. She was afraid Abby wasn't a good influence. She wasn't on my approved list of people I could interact with outside of the plant removal team, so it was an automatic no. It didn't matter how great or responsible or mature I said Abby was. Once Belén decided something, there was no changing her mind. I'd learned that the hard way.

My shoulders slumped in defeat. "Right."

I wished I could jump off Belén's ship onto a lifeboat and row myself to sunnier shores, but instead I went up to my room to work until dinner was ready. Except I was a glutton for punishment, so instead of opening the files I'd been working on, I decided to email Ashlyn first.

> Dear Ash,
>
> Me again. Hope things are going well at Blue Valley. Are you in summer classes? Anything interesting? Tea Parties for Beginners? The Art of Croquet?
>
> You're not missing much here in Arlington. I'm spending my days pulling plants out of the ground and my nights designing. I've gotten a couple new clients recently, so that's a plus. I'm making a book cover for this girl who writes science fiction. I'm starting with a black-and-white photo of the inside of a clock, all the gears and stuff. Thoughts?
>
> Belén is being her usual self. Tilly is ignoring me. Blanche, Belén's mom, is living with us, and she's pretty cool. My dad's gone again.
>
> Let me know how you are. Please.
>
> Be Well,
> Tate

She hadn't responded to my earlier email, which left a bitter taste in my mouth, but I still wanted to update her on what was going on with me. I had no idea if Ashlyn was coming back to Henderson in the fall, but part of me hoped so. Selfishly, because I wanted my friend back. Unselfishly, because I knew she'd probably need someone on her side if she did return. I used *Be Well* again because, the truth is, that's what I wished for her. I knew, no matter how mad I was at her—and that anger was beginning to fade ever so slowly—she was probably hurting too.

On my way back down to dinner, I heard Blanche and Tilly talking softly in the hallway. Not wanting to interrupt, I did what any good stepsister would do—hovered around the corner and eavesdropped.

"Of course they hurt, Abuela. That's part of dance."

"Yes, I suppose it comes with the territory. But I'm allowed to be concerned." Blanche paused. "I imagine it probably hurts less than if you cut off a toe or a heel, yes?" She chuckled. No response from Tilly, though. Did she not recognize a joke? "Sore feet aside, is it going well? It's hard to tell when I listen to you and your mother discuss things." Her keen sense of observation was apparently not limited to me.

I heard Tilly inhale slowly, like it took a great amount of effort. "I love it. Honestly, Abuela. All the sacrifices I make are worth it. I feel like I've really hit my stride this summer." There was a soft reverence in her voice, almost like a prayer. For a second, I forgot it was Tilly speaking; my breath caught in my throat.

"I'm glad, Matilda. If you're happy, I'm happy. You

just let me know if I can get you some ice for those feet, okay?"

Tilly giggled softly, a rare break in her stern façade. "I will. Thank you, Abuela."

"Te quiero."

"I love you too, Abuela."

After their footfalls disappeared, I peeked out from behind the corner in the hall, made sure the coast was clear, and followed them down to dinner, captivated by the strange display of affection from my stepsister.

Later that night, I put the finishing touches on Emily's book cover. I was pretty impressed with myself, given it was my first time making one.

Abby had recommended checking out recent steam-punk series she called "super popular" and the classic *The Time Machine* for inspiration. When she'd brought me her personal copies, dog-eared and creased, she said, "Treat them well. They're precious cargo." I had promised I would, and took them home to study.

Satisfied with the finished product, I sent the cover off to Emily. I checked my inbox again, which naturally was empty. I didn't know what else I could do. On one hand, if Ash was still having feelings about "the incident," then I couldn't expect much. I could picture her, hands hovering over her keyboard like mine had, trying to choose just the right words and then, being so unsure, talking herself out of replying at all. On the other hand, we were friends.

That had to count for something. We'd been friends for years, and I thought that should at least get me a reply to my inquiry about her health.

I didn't want to hold my breath, but I knew I would anyway.

Chapter 9

$\mathcal{F}$or the next week, every day was the same. Community service all day, work on my clients' projects in the evening at home or at the Schmidts', and then be subjected to the Belén and Tilly show at dinner. I was continually treated to Belén's running commentary of opinions as she drilled Tilly about the day's practice. The night Blanche went to a movie with a few of her new bunco friends was particularly painful.

"What were your lines like today?" Belén focused hawk-like eyes on her daughter, scrutinizing Tilly's shoulders and neck as she spooned rice into her mouth.

Like her mother, Tilly chewed each bite thirty times, so the pauses between her replies felt like eternities. They were both too focused on dance to give me a second glance, other than to ask me to pass the salt. Not that I wanted to join in the conversation, but it would have been nice to have been asked about my day too.

"My lines were perfect, Mama. As always."

"Good." Like a bullet from a gun. "Make sure you keep it that way."

As she did every night, Belén asked Tilly what her chances were for a solo at the end of workshop performance. And just as reliably, Tilly told her mother that she thought it was a lock. I needed to hand it to her. I had no idea if she was telling the truth, as her poker face rarely gave away anything, but I had a difficult time believing Tilly never had a bad day, a day where the odds of becoming the superstar of the District Ballet's summer program decreased.

Belén must have been feeling extra feisty, because she brought up college. I zoned out completely at that point because I could have recited her bullet-pointed agenda items, I'd heard them so many times. If Belén got to choose, Tilly would go to a super-selective university and then to a top law school, all while maintaining a spot in a prestigious dance company and touring the world. When that line of discussion arrived at the table, as graceful as a moose on a bobsled, even Tilly had trouble keeping a straight face and acting like her mother's vision was humanly possible. She just nodded and kept her mouth shut.

I thought Belén might have sent a reminder my way about signing up for the SAT prep class Tilly took last summer, but nothing. Nada.

Since no one was paying attention to me, I got up to refill my iced tea. Feeling charitable, I refilled Tilly's empty glass as well.

She looked up at me with surprise in her brown eyes. "Thank you, Tatum."

"You're welcome." I tried to smile at her, but she looked down again before I could make the corners of my mouth lift. I smiled anyway, a little proud of myself.

After the meal, to my room I went with only novels and my computer for company. I was grateful for the time to work on my design projects, but even I had my limits on how much lonely I could stand.

Which is how I got suckered into sneaking out with Abby to Hunter's band's practice.

What are you doing tonight?

An hour after I'd pulled myself into my shell, Abby sent me a text as I was attempting to drown out the white noise in my head by putting on my headphones and listening to some Sarah Jarosz, which I may or may not have downloaded on SK's recommendation.

Sitting in my jail. I mean my room.

No you're not. You're coming with me to see the Frisson.

What exactly is the Frisson?

Hunter's band. They have practice tonight. Go with me to see them.

Right. You're forgetting about the warden and the mileage report.

Belén's rejection of my perfectly innocent request for
dinner with Abby still smarted.

No problem. Go to the pet house and I'll pick you up.
Send me the address.

I was tempted. I missed fun. I missed people who weren't
assigned to be with me or felt nothing but disappointment
or disdain for me, depending on the day. I missed positive
attention from humans. Not that I minded the hamster love
I got from Princess Sweetheart, but it only went so far to
boost my self-esteem.

Let me think about it.

Abby's solution was simple and would probably work,
unless Belén followed me or had spies around the neighborhood. If I told her the Schmidts called last minute and
needed me to come over, she probably wouldn't question
it. And if Abby picked me up, that would take care of the
odometer issue. But on the off chance something went
wrong, my head would be rolling for sure.

I idly opened my laptop and considered the work I
should be doing. Hunter's bandmates agreed to me making
a sample flyer for them, and they'd talked with the guy in
charge of Sol Jam about advertising that too. Apparently
Owen thought it was "an inspired idea," and hoped he
could make the event bigger than ever this year. I was
supposed to bring something to show Hunter to our next
plant-pulling session. As I stared at the screen, my eyes
unfocused, and I zoned out until the ding of my email
brought me back to reality. My chest seized up when I saw

the sender's name; my hand dipped into my pocket and gripped my house key, the teeth biting into my palm.

> Tatum,
>
>> While I appreciate your attempt at diffusing the tension between us, I need you to understand that I am still very upset with you for turning me in. I can't stop you from emailing me, but don't expect me to reply again. I'm doing my best to adjust to this new life that was thrust upon me, and I am not at a point where I'm ready to deal with my old one, and that includes you. If/when I come to that place, I will let you know.
>
>> Best,
>> Ashlyn

I had to remind myself to breathe when I got to the end of the email. Definitely not what I had been expecting—the email itself, or Ashlyn's response. I reread it three more times before I could tear myself away from the screen. Okay, so she was still mad at me, and she implied I was disloyal. That was fine. I could understand that, and even see from her point of view how that was true.

The fourth read through, I laughed. Her word choices were so much like her father's: terse and professionally snarky. Maybe she'd consulted with her dad on what to say. She'd never use those words in the real world. On the fifth read, it dawned on me that even though she was dismissing me, she was also giving me a tiny shred of hope. She said *if/when*, which left the door cracked, a bit, for me to slide back in. With that revelation wrapping its claws around my heart and shaking it, I texted Abby back.

Pick me up in 30 minutes.

I needed to channel the adrenaline surge that was gliding through my system, and music sounded like a good outlet. I printed my sample posters and shoved them into my bag. I left a note for Belén, who had just left to go shopping for new leotards with Tilly, saying I'd gotten a last-minute babysitting request, with my car's mileage written at the bottom, natch, and told Blanche, who had just returned from her movie and was stretched out in the basement with an afghan and a cup of tea, that I was going to take care of the girls. She looked up from her romance novel, the kind with a ripped, shirtless warrior in a kilt on the cover, winked at me, and told me to have a good time. I shook my head in disbelief, walking back up the stairs. I swear the woman was psychic. Or my Patronus. Blanche always sensed exactly what I needed. She somehow knew what I was up to no matter how sneaky I thought I was being. And cheered me on.

At the Schmidts', I dealt with the animals and blew Gus a kiss goodbye as I dashed out the door and into Abby's car, which tonight surprisingly was of the muscle variety. I slid my hand over the black vinyl of the dashboard as she pulled out into the street. "What is this fine piece of machinery?"

"Oh, you like it, do you? This is my brother's baby. He's grounded tonight, so his loss is my gain. She's a 1968 Camaro."

"That means nothing to me."

"Pretty much all you need to know is that she's a classic and that he rebuilt her himself, so I must drive slower than your grandmother, but we'll get there eventually."

I snickered. "I think my stepgrandmother might actually love this car, and would drive it like she was on the autobahn."

"Right on. So what convinced you to come tonight? I thought you were chained to your bed. I know you didn't ask for permission."

I bounced my heel on the floor mat and studied my silver sandals, knotted too tightly at my ankles. "I just needed some company, I guess."

Abby did an admirable job of staying straight on the road while still giving me a suspicious look. "No. You don't get to do that. You were all keyed up when you got in the car, and your voice just plummeted to the floor. You're also ticking like you're anxious. What happened? Because I know something did."

I mashed my lips together. Curse Abby and her journalist's observation skills, even though I knew it wasn't hard to pick up on the vibe I was sending out. My voice came out shaky and quiet. "Ashlyn emailed me back."

"And?"

I set my head on the headrest behind me and closed my eyes. I recited the email, word for biting word. I'd read it so many times, I had it memorized, burned into my brain for all eternity, or at least until the next crisis.

"Shut the front door. What is her problem? I mean, I get that she's mad, but you are so not the person she should be mad at. You did exactly what any self-respecting human being would do in that unfair situation. She should be livid with her subhuman boyfriend—or ex, I hope—and direct all her righteous attitude to the city jail."

I just blinked at her. "Can I fire my lawyer and hire you instead?"

"Sure. Can I be paid the same salary?" We laughed together. "And signing off with 'best'? Seriously? Who uses that besides snobs and twits?"

I yelped with laughter. "I love you for saying that. That was my favorite part! I can't stand 'best.' It makes me want to gouge my eyes out."

"Am I right? The worst way to end a letter." Then her voice took on a more somber tone. "I'm so sorry, Tate. I guess she's still processing."

"That's a good way to put it." I wondered if Chase was processing too, from his jail cell, hopefully with a scary cellmate. Probably not.

"So, are you going to respond to her?"

I shrugged. "Probably. At least she wrote back. I take it as a good sign that she wants to scold me, but she also doesn't want me to forget about her."

"That's messed up." Abby shook her head.

"Yeah, it is what it is. She's my friend. Hopefully, we'll get past it. And if we don't, we don't." Sometimes I even impressed myself with my ability to stay calm when all I really wanted to do was scream or cry or punch a hole in something.

"It is what it is," Abby echoed, trying the words on for size and nodding slowly.

At Hunter's house, the garage door was wide open, with questionable noises sailing out into the night.

"Are you sure this is a good idea?" I whispered.

"Any time with Hunter is a good idea, in my world."

"Fair enough."

Inside the garage, Hunter was standing front and center, tuning an electric guitar. A guy I knew from school—a senior, I think—sat behind a drum kit that had seen better days, and another guy, totally unfamiliar, was wielding a bass like a weapon, a look of contempt on his face.

"This isn't working," the bass player grumbled as we approached, setting his instrument down dramatically on the stand at his feet. Hunter looked up, and Abby waved. He nodded at us and gestured with his chin for us to take a seat in the two folding chairs that were off to the side, but still in plain view of the band. We sat.

"We have to practice, even if Shay isn't here. There are only a few weeks left till Sol Jam." The drummer peered over a cymbal at the bass player, like a parent reminding a child to do his chores. The bass player rolled his eyes, and Hunter continued to tune his guitar, ignoring the other two.

Abby and I looked at each other nervously. It felt like we'd walked into the middle of something we weren't supposed to hear. I was just contemplating grabbing Abby's elbow and dragging her out of there when she stood up and squared her shoulders.

"Hi, guys, or should I call you the Frisson?" She laughed too loudly and smiled too brightly. I cringed for her. "Um, I'm Abby Gold, and I write for the *Henderson*

Herald. I'm sure Hunter has told you about the article I'm going to write." Bass and Drums looked at her blankly. "Right. And this is Tatum Elsea; she's designing the Sol Jam poster, and if I can convince her, she's going to help me with the article." I raised an eyebrow to no one in particular. It wasn't me who needed convincing.

"Hey," I said, and tried to smile.

Hunter finally stopped messing with his guitar. "This is Paolo." He pointed to the guy behind the drums. He waved his drumsticks at us and smiled. "And that grump in the corner is Kyle. Ignore him." Kyle said nothing. No smile, no wave, no friendly gesture at all.

"Our fourth member, Shay, is unfortunately on vacation," Paolo said.

I would probably need a vacation if I were in the middle of an entire summer of band practice with Kyle too. His sour attitude definitely needed to be tempered by some sand and a cool ocean breeze. I could think of a few people I'd like to take a vacation from as well. If that was Shay's intention, she sounded like someone I'd get along with.

Kyle took his bass back up and started picking out a line. Hunter and Paolo exchanged a look that affirmed Kyle was the timekeeper and perhaps tyrant of the band. The boys launched into something that sounded a little bit rock, a little bit folk, and a little bit something all on its own. Even without a microphone, Hunter's lead vocals cut through the instrumentals like an emotional laser. The lyrics spoke about the possibility of love, of wondering what might come next, and I fully believed that Hunter knew just what that felt like as he sang.

Kyle and Paolo were uber-focused on their instruments, concentrating on playing the right notes and keeping the beat, but I couldn't help but notice Hunter's eyes stayed on Abby. A quick glance to my left confirmed that Abby was waffling back and forth between watching Hunter sing and pretending to take notes about the performance in her journalist's steno pad. I checked myself before I laughed at the rows of hearts and stars she'd drawn instead. Good for them. I wonder which one of them would crack first. I hoped it would happen soon, before my feeling like an unwanted third wheel set in.

By the fourth song, I'd relaxed enough to start singing along with their bluesy arrangement of a pop song that'd achieved overplayed-on-the-radio status months ago. Abby pulled me out of my chair and we did a clumsy jitterbug, twirling each other around the dusty concrete floor of the Hansen garage. By the time the song ended, my sides ached from laughing so hard. As Abby dropped my hands, I looked up at the guys. They were all grinning like clowns at us, which I assumed was a good thing. At least they weren't pointing and laughing.

"Do you ladies want to be our official fly girls?" Paolo stood up from behind his drums and started making some jerky movements with knee bends and robot-like arms. I covered my mouth and stifled a laugh.

"I think our moves were better than that." Abby put a hand on her hip in mock annoyance.

Hunter swept his hair to the side. "You could be plants in the audience during Sol Jam. If a whole crowd of people got up and danced during our show, that would be awesome."

Kyle nodded in agreement. "And then it won't just be Shay acting like a fool on stage."

"What does Shay do?" I asked.

"Ignore Kyle," Hunter interjected. "Shay just likes to have fun. Stands up while playing the piano, dances around, people seem to like it." He shrugged. "Generally, the audience is into it," Hunter said a little louder in Kyle's direction. He leaned closer to us and whispered, loudly, "Some people don't have much of a sense of humor."

"Noted. So that was really fun. Thanks for letting us crash."

"Thanks for risking it." Hunter half-smiled at me. He'd set his guitar down in its stand and taken a few steps closer to Abby. "Do you want to, um, talk about your notes, Ab?"

"Oh, sure." She blushed so red, her cheeks looked purple in the fluorescent lighting of the garage. She parked herself back in her chair, and Hunter sat down in mine.

"I'll just go use the restroom," I said to no one in particular, and booked it into the house. After finishing up, I came back out, and smiled when I saw Abby and Hunter both hunched over, talking like no one else was in the room. Kyle was fiddling with his bass again, but Paolo beamed up at me from his stool as I approached.

"So you're making our poster, right?"

I nodded. "It looks that way. Which reminds me, I have some samples in the car. Do you want to look at them?"

"Yeah, definitely."

He followed me to Abby's brother's car, jaw practically dragging on the ground when he saw it. "This is yours?"

"Uh, no. I am not to be trusted."

He looked at me quizzically, but didn't say anything more. I pulled out my hobo bag and handed him the samples. Paolo studied them for several minutes, and the longer he took, the more my heart raced and the harder I gripped the car door. I didn't think I'd ever get used to people looking at my work and deciding if they wanted to use it to promote themselves. Letting me help them. I wasn't sure I wanted to get used to it.

When my knuckles were fully white and aching, Paolo lifted his eyes to meet mine and handed me back the mock-ups. "These are awesome!"

I inhaled with relief. "Thanks," I said shyly.

"I think I like this one for us." He gestured to the poster in my left hand. I'd superimposed a fun, vintage-looking font with the band's name and the information about Sol Jam over a close-up photograph of grains of wood. It looked like a weathered barrel or the floor of an old-timey saloon. Now that I'd heard the Frisson's sound, I had to agree with Paolo that it was a good fit.

"I'm glad you like it." I smiled so wide, I thought my cheeks might explode with the force of expansion.

"Can I hang on to these?" He reached for the posters again. "We can talk about them together when Shay gets back, and then we'll let you know."

"Definitely." I craned my neck to see if Abby and Hunter were still engrossed in their private conversation, and caught them just in time to see him squeeze her shoulder and stand up to go back to his guitar.

"Looks like they're getting started again," I said to Paolo. "You guys are really good, by the way."

He looked genuinely pleased at my compliment. "Thank you. We have a lot of fun. Wait till you hear us when Shay's back. The piano really kicks it up a notch."

"I hope I get to hear it one day," I said, a string of sadness stitching its way into my voice.

"What does that mean?"

"I'm not really here," I admitted, putting air quotes on my words.

"Say no more. I understand. Parent trouble?"

"You have no idea." Paolo raised his fist, and I brought mine to meet it. We shared a knowing smile between us as Abby approached. "Did you get everything you needed?" I asked her, trying desperately to hold in the wink that wanted to bust out.

She blushed. "I did, thanks." She waved at Paolo and kept on trucking to the car.

I shrugged at him and followed. "See you . . . some-time . . ." I trailed off. He waved back and went into the garage.

Moments later, Abby joined me at the car with pink cheeks and a silly grin on her face. She was still smiling as we slid into the vinyl seats and she revved the engine.

"So what were you and Hunter talking about all secret-like over there?" I poked Abby in the shoulder as she backed out of the Hansens' driveway.

"He, uh, wanted to see the notes I'd taken about their songs."

I tried not to laugh at her and her nonexistent notes. "And what did he think of those notes?"

"I sat on them and told him I had everything I needed up here." She tapped on her forehead.

"Smooth."

"Right? So we talked about doing a small piece on each band member, their background and inspiration, that kind of thing. Then a longer piece on how they met, how they work together, who does the arranging and all that. And obviously a lot of pictures and a bit on Sol Jam itself. Hunter was pretty psyched. He gave me his phone number so we can collaborate." By the time she said "phone number," her smile had increased threefold and was creeping dangerously close to her ears.

"Took him long enough," I said. She just kept on smiling.

When she dropped me back off at the Schmidts' house, it was right when I would normally be leaving from my "job."

"Perfect timing."

Abby gave me a sly look. "I had the *best* time tonight." She looked me square in the eyes when she said *best*. A lightbulb went off as I realized she was poking fun at Ashlyn's use of the worst valediction known to man.

"Oh, I heard what you did there. You are definitely the *best*," and I returned the pointed gaze. We both cracked up and I sucked in a breath, feeling relaxed and something that felt suspiciously like happy. Abby and I high-fived, then I ducked in the house to double check on the animals and headed home.

When I stopped in the kitchen for a drink before going to bed, I jumped as I turned away from the sink to find Belén sitting silently at the kitchen table, staring so intensely at me that I thought I might combust. Her long fingers were wrapped around a mug of tea, and she spoke in a low, dangerous voice.

"Did you have a nice evening with the Schmidt girls?" She'd never once asked me about Kate and Maya in all the years I'd been sitting for them.

"It was fine."

"Perhaps, since you had a fine evening, Tatum, you'd care to explain why you were at an address that is not the Schmidts' house for quite a long time."

I froze. "Excuse me? Are you having me followed now?" The frustration—and embarrassment at being caught—that exploded in my chest threatened to knock me down, or fly out of me in the form of molten lava or lightning. I did my best to lock my knees and purse my lips instead, so she wouldn't know what was going on inside my head.

"There's this wonderful invention called a Global Positioning System. The nice people who sold us your cell phone had the foresight to install one in every model for occasions such as lost phone, lost child, things like that." Belén was being sarcastic, something she only did when she was really angry. Dad got quiet; Belén thought she was a comedian.

My arms and legs buzzed with adrenaline. "You GPSed me? Why would you do that?" I was almost crying. I knew without looking that my face was red, and I hoped that Blanche and Tilly couldn't hear us arguing.

"I've been keeping track of you each time you leave the house. Someone needed to make sure you were following the rules."

"Did that awful parenting blog you love recommend it?" I lashed out.

Belén pursed her lips tightly. A twitch at the corner of her right eye gave me my answer. Hurt bubbled up in my throat, that she would think so little of me, and was quickly replaced with shame because I'd proven her right.

"That is so wrong," I whispered, mostly to myself.

Belén didn't respond with words, but by picking up the phone and dialing slowly, each button sounding its low beep. She paused and then spoke in her professional, clipped voice. "She's home. Yes. I did. Sure, here she is." She handed the cordless to me and said, "It's your father." Of course it was.

I took the phone without looking at her, wiped my angry-tear eyes, and brought it to my ear. "Hi, Dad."

He said nothing for a moment, and I knew I was in real trouble. "Tatum, did you lie about where you were tonight?" I'd already been caught, so trying to get out of it was pointless.

"Yes."

"Where were you?" I could barely hear him, and I knew it wasn't the long-distance connection, but his disappointment making his voice fade away.

"I went with my friend Abby Gold to see our classmate Hunter Hansen and his band practice."

"I see." Did he really? I doubted it. "So you felt that going to band practice was more important than proving yourself reliable and responsible?"

I sighed into the phone. "Dad, I've been cooped up in the house or sweating my behind off pulling plants for weeks now. I thought I deserved a little reprieve, and I knew there was no way anyone here"—I glared in Belén's direction—"was going to give me permission, so I went. It was wrong. I know that. But I did it anyway."

And I'm not sorry, I added silently. Well, I was sorry I had lied and let them down. But I wasn't sorry that I'd had fun for the first time in ages, or that I was making a new friend to start to fill that Ashlyn-sized hole in my chest.

"I see," Dad repeated. This was the moment of truth as far as I was concerned. Was he going to let Belén's influence completely zombie-fy him, or would he come back from the brink of destruction?

"Tatum, I really want to trust you, and I know it's unpleasant to have to refuse an offer from a friend, but tonight, you chose the unsafe option. What if something had happened to you? What if you'd gotten a flat tire or had an accident? No one knew where you were. You may think this isn't a big deal, but I refuse to compromise when it comes to your safety."

"I had my phone! I would have called if I needed help. Or Abby would have," I protested.

Dad sighed into the receiver. "Your mother and I—"

I winced at his slip. "Stop right there, Dad. She is not, has never been, and never will be my mother." I slammed the phone down on the table, hoping it disconnected.

"Tatum." Belén remained calm and collected, hands clasped around her mug. "I think we should—" But I didn't want to hear what she thought. Dad had made it perfectly clear that I was incapable of making the correct decision, and I didn't need her to reiterate it for me.

"I think we've talked enough." I stared at her, half-daring her to challenge me. I expected her to stand up to her full height and try to intimidate me, but she just sat there, knuckles growing paler the longer she gripped her mug. For a moment, it seemed her face had begun to droop, and I was sure her eye was twitching again. There was no way Belén could be bothered by what just went down. Right? I shook my head. Impossible.

Chapter 10

I couldn't be in the same room with her, so I left. When I reached my room, I slammed the door so hard that the walls shook, and I heard a loud thud in the next room, like something had fallen and broken. It felt like I had done an awful lot of door-slamming this summer.

I knew my dad would call back and want to talk again. I told myself I wouldn't take his call. Not until he came home, if I could last that long. Maybe this was a test to see which one of us would crack first.

I opened my laptop to check my email, hoping for a distraction, but the only message was from my dad, sent two minutes ago. Great. I looked at it cautiously, as if the words might physically hurt me.

> Sweetheart,
>> I love you. No matter what, we'll get through this.
>>> Chin up,
>>> Dad

Was it easier for him to be optimistic because he was so far away? Because there was no other way to wrap my head around his words. I kept making the wrong choices, and he and Belén kept adding them up. I squeezed my eyes shut, releasing a few tears and a low, guttural growl.

I flung myself onto my bed. The covers flew up around me and a pillow fell to the floor. The tears pooling in my eyes leaked down my cheeks, and ugly sobs sent shudders through my body, right down to my feet. I shoved my face into the remaining pillow so Blanche or Tilly didn't hear me wailing. I cried until my pillow was damp with salty tears and the sheet stuck to my face. I cried until my lungs ached from the heaving and my body was sore from the stress. I remained splayed on the bed, submitting to the exhaustion.

My email dinged, and my eyes jolted open. I rolled over and checked my phone to see it was just past four a.m. I must have dozed off. I stood up, dizzy for a moment, and walked to my desk. My email inbox was open on the screen when I typed in my password, and there, to my surprise, was an email from SK.

> Hi Tate,
>
> Sorry for the delayed response to our last email. I'm actually in Ireland with my family right now and haven't had technology for a while. It's driving me to the brink, especially since my dad keeps teasing me about how "kids these days" can't go anywhere without checking our phones every five seconds.

I snorted. I'd just confirmed that theory myself by responding to the notification so quickly.

> So I know we'd talked about having some kind of media files on the site. I have videos from school concerts, but I don't think they really represent who I am. I will have better stuff though, probably by the end of the summer, so stay tuned. I did, however, manage to steal my cousin's laptop and record a couple of songs for you. I had to save them onto a flash drive and walk ten miles uphill in the snow to an internet cafe to send you this email. Okay, maybe not that far, but my grandparents are still living in the Stone Age. Anyway, let me know what you think. They're some of my favorite pieces—I hope that's obvious when you listen.
>
> Out of curiosity, do you have a lot of clients? Is business going well? You don't have to tell me. But I hope it is.
>
> Le gach beannacht,
> SK
>
> P.S.—that means "with every blessing," which is cheesy, but it's how my grandmother signs letters. A little bit of Ireland for you.

For the first time since I got home, I smiled. How was it that a total stranger, someone I'd never met, who only knew me from the words and images I'd shared across the internet, cared enough to ask how something important to me was going? And how was it that the people who supposedly knew me—my best friend, my father, my stepmother, my stepsister—struggled to think one tiny, positive thought about me?

> Dear SK,

Because what he'd written was dear to me.

> Thank you for the music. I'm going to listen right now, as I'm getting ready for bed. Had a rough night, so I'm hoping hearing you play will pick me up a bit. I'm jealous that you're off in a magical place and I'm stuck here at home, nowhere to go. I'd love to visit Ireland one day. Or anywhere, actually. My dad travels all over the world for work; maybe wanderlust is genetic. Send me a picture? Maybe we can put it on your site.
>
> Since I don't have a clever valediction in a foreign language to one-up you, I'm just going to say good night.
>
> Tate

I sent it off and immediately downloaded SK's cello files to my computer. Just as I was hovering over the file titled *Bach Chaconne*, ready to click and listen, my email dinged again.

> Why did you have a rough night? Do I need to make a phone call and have someone's kneecaps destroyed? Because I could do that, you know.

I laughed out loud. What would Belén do if a hit man showed up at the door with a lead pipe? Probably tell him that he'd brought an ineffective weapon.

Not to pry, but I'm an excellent listener, er, typist,
and I have another fifteen minutes of time paid for.
Feel free to vent, but only if you want to. No pressure.

Kwaheri,
SK

P.S.—that one's Swahili. It means goodbye, not sure
if it's appropriate for a letter; I never did pay enough
attention when my dad was trying to teach me.

His dad spoke Swahili? Interesting. Did he do the same
kind of thing as my dad, or had he grown up speaking it?
My dad knew enough Swahili to get by in the countries he
frequented where it was spoken. In fact, he knew enough
of most major world languages to get by, since it was pretty
much required for work. It made me wish I was better
with words. I took boring and useless Latin because Belén
thought it would help me on my SATs.

I replied right away.

So are both of your parents immigrants? That's
cool. My stepmom immigrated, but she's pretty
much the opposite of cool.

I snuck out of the house when I wasn't supposed
to. Got caught. Got lectured at by said stepmom.
Kinda deserved it, but still. Though the knight-in-
shining-armor offer is tempting. Rain check?

No point in spilling my guts to a stranger. I didn't
think my fingers had the energy to type it all out anyway.

P.S. Where's my picture?

I sent the email and changed into my pajamas. The worn flannel of the pants and the nubby cotton T-shirt provided another layer of comfort, like a fabric bandage for my smarting soul. I sat back down at the laptop to find the most beautiful photograph of rolling emerald hills, dotted with a weathered wooden fence and stones marking a footpath.

> Sorry, I forgot! Better late than never, right? I actually took this yesterday, intending to send it to you for the site. Great minds think alike. It's the field at the end of my grandparents' road. Rural doesn't begin to cover this place. I thought you'd appreciate the green.
>
> Yes, my dad's from Kenya originally. He came here for college and never left. I think meeting my mom probably had a lot to do with it, though. That's a story for another day—my time is up, unfortunately.
>
> I hope you get some sleep and that whatever you snuck out for was worth it. I've found it usually is.
>
> SK

I looked at the photograph again; it made my heart hurt. I wished more than anything that I could teleport myself somewhere peaceful and quiet, where people smiled and laughed instead of keeping themselves buttoned so tight they choked themselves.

I fantasized about a family vacation, only with a warped version of the family I actually had. My dad was still my dad, because in all honesty, he was great the way

he was. Blanche was there, in all her contradictory love-
liness, only kicked up a notch. She wore feather boas and
tiaras, the eccentric grandmother who pinched cute boys'
butts and spouted kooky advice to strangers. Tilly spoke
on a regular basis with everyone, including me, and she
and I together eerily looked like we were friends. And
Belén smiled—a real smile that reached her eyes—gave
hugs when someone cried, and laughed full and una-
bashed when something funny happened. She let go and
didn't bother to care who was looking when she did. The
five of us rode a red double-decker bus around a random
European city, phones out snapping pictures, smacking
each other on the shoulders to look at the sites we passed,
and bickering warm-heartedly over where to go next.

I sighed loudly, knowing that's all it was, a fantasy. But
that didn't stop me from wishing it could be true anyway.
Intent on listening to some quiet music to relax me as I
drifted off to sleep again, I put my laptop on the bed next
to me, slid in between the cool sheets, and pressed play on
"Chaconne" as my head hit the pillow.

The first strains of the cello were hesitant and timid,
like it was afraid to show itself due to a small case of stage
fright. I waited patiently for it to become louder, like a
parent waits for a scared child to gain confidence, coaxing
him out of his shell. As the volume picked up, so did the
emotion, and suddenly I was awash in a sea of sounds. If
those first few notes were trickles, there was now a raging
ocean of crashing waves, washing over my head one after
another. I'd been half expecting something that was just
a deeper violin, but this cello had a mind of its own. The

sound was rich and saturated with molasses and electricity. It was like a human voice, a melancholy song of longing, pleading with the listener to ease his frustration. People say there's a fine line between pleasure and pain, and that was exactly the message this cello was sending out. Even though the sadness was undeniable, there was also an underlying sensuality, a slow-burning passion reaching out, begging for the listener to hear the want, the need.

As I lay there listening, I knew there was no hope of me relaxing. The tears that had magically disappeared at the words on the screen came back with a vengeance as the notes filled the air and invaded my head. Scalding my skin, they dripped down my cheeks silently. I cried for the girl whose voice remained unheard, who did her best to be good but didn't always get it right. I cried for the girl constantly trying to forge a connection, to find someone who took her at face value and didn't ask her to be something she wasn't. I cried for the doors that had closed and cried for the ones that might never open. I cried out of want, out of thirst for something nameless, my heart beating itself into a frenzy, my body completely boneless beneath the sheets, now heated and damp.

When the song ended, I couldn't move. My face was slick, tears clinging to my eyelashes as I stared at the ceiling, seeing nothing. I willed my breathing to slow until I was calm and sated. It felt like I'd just run a marathon, the exhaustion was so overwhelming. I closed my eyes and marveled at how magical it was that I could feel all of that, an eruption of emotion, from a song. And if the song could communicate all of that sadness and yearning, what did it say about the musician breathing life into that song? What had SK been thinking that allowed him to play with such fervor?

The sorrow fled as quickly as it had arrived, moving over for a meddling curiosity. I sat up and opened my email once more.

> That completely wrecked me. Bravo.
>
> T

Chapter 11

Despite the hurricane that had passed through our house, the punishment remained the same. There wasn't really anything more Belén could inflict on me, within reasonable levels of human decency, anyway. I imagined her feeling smug and justified in her previous assessment of me. Tatum Elsea was trouble and Belén Castillo-Elsea knew it all along. I wondered if this confirmation helped her sleep at night.

Because Belén was all about keeping commitments, she didn't tell me to quit my "babysitting" of the Schmidt girls. I think she'd considered it, I'm sure she had, but knowing how her brain worked, she probably assumed that it would stir up more dirt than she was willing to deal with. She probably thought it was stressful enough to keep me in the house and away from respectable friends for a school-related project. Same song, different day.

For the next few days, I didn't even come out of my room to watch TV Land with Blanche or exchange chilly silences with Tilly. I read books, occasionally flipped through the SAT study guide that had mysteriously appeared on my bed, worked while listening to SK play his cello on repeat, and usually cried myself to sleep. Sometimes I was ragey. Sometimes I wallowed. Most of the time, though, I felt defeated.

On the mornings I wasn't doing my community service, when I became too restless to lie in bed anymore, I'd roll lazily out from under the covers, wrap myself in a Henderson hoodie, and sit at my desk to open my laptop. I usually craved a cup of peppermint tea and hoped Blanche might psychically connect with my thoughts and bring me one, but she never did. I scanned through my email inboxes, sifting through spam, college mailing list blasts, and coupons, hoping a new potential client would seek me out.

One Saturday morning at the beginning of August, someone did.

> Dear TLC Design,
>
> My name is Matilda Castillo, and I am currently a rising senior at McIntosh High School for the Performing Arts in Arlington, VA.

Wait, what? My evil stepsister was trying to hire me? This was too precious.

> This summer, I was selected to take part in a unique opportunity for elite dancers with the District Ballet Company's summer intensive program.

She was more of Belén's clone than I'd realized. *Unique opportunity? Elite?* I didn't know anyone else my age who would say those things. I couldn't believe that she and I had lived in the same house for ten years and grown up worlds apart.

> As a result of this program, I've discovered a passion for contemporary dance, and want to create a personal website that highlights the work I've done this summer to hone this skill.

My eyes bugged out of my head. Hold the phone— contemporary dance? I reread the sentence several times to make sure that's what she'd actually written. As far as anyone at home knew, Tilly was dancing the perfect *pas de deux* in her black leotard, pink tights, shiny toe shoes, and expertly crafted bun, vying for the title of queen of the ballet. I called up my knowledge of a very popular reality TV show that involved prima ballerinas competing against breakdancers for some insane amount of money and a contract for a music video that wouldn't ever see the light of day; I'd seen it a time or two with Ashlyn. Or ten or fifteen, but who's counting. I remember really feeling invested for about three episodes in this one girl who danced like her life depended on getting through the next motion, the next leap or thrust. She chose painfully emotional songs, and her choreography always mimicked whatever feeling the music was conveying. Her movements were jerky and sharp, her toes were flexed instead of pointed, she rolled and writhed, and sometimes there was an ugliness to her body, but her face always told a story. She was a contemporary dancer. That's what Tilly had a passion for? I would never have put the ice queen and passion in the same sentence. Or zip code. Who was this person?

> I'd like to make a site I can send to colleges that would serve as an art supplement, so it would need to be created using the standards set forth by the selective universities I'll be applying to in the fall.

Ah, there she was again.

> I've taken a look at your portfolio, and the idea of a personalized questionnaire used to determine the best fit for me and my needs is appealing.

I aim to please. You're welcome. Glad I could meet your needs.

> If you could please send whatever forms or paperwork you need me to complete to get started, I would greatly appreciate it. I look forward to working with you.
>
> V/R,
> Matilda

What the heck was V/R? A quick google told me it was an abbreviation for "very respectfully."

"How is that respectful?" I muttered to myself. I thought that maybe writing out the words you intended the recipient to see, instead of using an acronym, might actually send a message of respect, but what did I know. Maybe discovering new passions with elite dancers and honing your skills made you an expert on respect.

I stared at the screen wondering how to handle this. I could treat it like a burden, just one more opportunity to bask in Tilly's superior achievements and life choices, or I could treat Tilly's request like a gift. A chance to get a peek inside her head. Or maybe, just maybe, a shot at melting some of the ice wedged between us. I wasn't going to hold my breath on that one, but you never knew. Not a difficult decision after all.

I smiled to myself, printed out a copy of my client preferences survey—complete with the TLC Design logo right smack at the top—and took myself down the hall to Tilly's bedroom. I realized that giving Tilly my survey, blowing my cover and revealing that I had a secret business, was a risky move, but I was banking on the fact that she wanted her secret kept quiet even more than I did mine. Plus, I really wanted to see how she would react when she figured out I was TLC. Giddiness practically leaking out my ears, I raised my fist to knock just as she opened the door and slammed right into me.

"What are you doing?" she spat, and rubbed her forehead, which was turning bright pink where we'd collided.

"I just wanted to give you something you asked me for." I held the client questionnaire out to her with both hands and smiled sweetly.

I wish I'd thought to bring a camera and record the moment for posterity. Tilly was always the kind of girl who, even though she was reserved and introverted and unfailingly polite, you knew had a lot going on under the surface. If you took a look inside her head, you'd probably see five mice running overtime on their little treadmill wheels just to keep up with all the thoughts she had.

When she saw what I was offering her, it was like those mice didn't just stop running, they fell off the wheels altogether, rendered immobile from shock. Her face blanched with fear. Fear of disappointing her mother, perhaps? Nope. It was the pure fear of being caught. The same look that jerkface Chase Massey had for a millisecond when the security guard approached my car at Mason's, right before he turned into a sad, skinny version of the not-so-incredible Hulk. I would never forget it.

I held the papers out again. "You wanted this, right? I got your email a few minutes ago. Figured it was easier to deliver it by hand. A nice, personal touch. Shows I care, don't you think?" I dared her to respond, my eyes flashing their challenge.

Tilly hesitated and then whispered, "You're TLC?" I could see her putting the puzzle pieces of my name and the company name together. At least one mouse must have gotten back on the wheel. There was disbelief in her tone, and maybe it was the fact we'd smacked heads a moment before, but I thought I might have seen the Ghost of Impressed pass over her. Tilly had always been so preoccupied with her own activities and commitments that she never really paid much attention to mine.

"At your service." I gave her a mock curtsy. "So, would you fill that out ASAP so I can get going on your portfolio site? You know, the one you want so you can feature your passion for, what was it again?" I put a finger to the corner of my lips. "Oh, that's right, contemporary dance."

Tilly grabbed my arm and hauled me into her room, reminding me never to underestimate the strength of a dancer, and shut the door behind us. "You cannot tell my mother." Her face was inches from mine, so close I could feel her breath warm on my skin.

"Chill out." I took a few steps away. I hadn't meant to scare her, only tease her a little bit. "Why would I tell Helicopter Mom of the Year about this?"

"Seriously?" The look of disbelief was back.

"Seriously. You're my client, or you wanted to be, anyway. If I tell Belén about you, you lose your portfolio, I potentially lose my business. Probably not the smartest move."

All the mice regained momentum as Tilly considered my logic. Visible relief draped itself over her cheeks and her shoulders, and she sat down on her bed, much more relaxed than ten seconds prior. "You're not going to tell her?"

I shook my head.

"But you hate me." She was matter-of-fact.

"I don't hate you."

She put a hand on her hip and quirked an eyebrow skyward, managing to look menacing even though she was sitting and looking up at me.

"I don't," I repeated. "I can't say I always like you"—this made me laugh and made her look more annoyed—"but you can't deny that we don't really know each other." I pointed to the survey. "Case in point. If you and I talked or had any kind of actual relationship, there's probably a chance you would have told me about your new, um, passion."

She considered this. "Maybe. Maybe not."

"Maybe not," I conceded. "Look, I'm not going to say anything and I'm not going to ask you about it, unless you want to tell me, but if you want me to do the website, I really do need you to fill out the questions. It helps me do my job." She didn't respond, but her eyes tilted down. "Do you still want me to do it?"

"Yes. I need it." I didn't know if she meant the website, the dancing, who knows. But I wasn't going to push her buttons anymore. She was already clearly in distress. It occurred to me that feeling anxiety about keeping secrets from her mother was the first thing Tilly and I had ever had in common.

"All right, then. Get me your answers and I'll get started." I gave her a curt nod, opened the door, and went back to my room, still a little baffled by what had just happened. In the course of a few minutes, I'd learned more about my stepsister than I had in years of living under the same roof. And I wasn't totally sure what that said about me, her, or us.

❤

Back in my room, I sat, holding my new discovery like a brand-new baby; something that needed to be guarded, something delicate and breakable. Partnering with Tilly was a huge risk, for both of us. In a matter of seconds, our entire relationship—thin as it was—had changed completely. It was shocking what uncovering clandestine information could do to one's outlook on life. One wrong move and the whole web would rip and come crashing down. I hoped she could keep up her end of the bargain. I hoped I could too.

Instinct took over, and I did what I've always done when something is trying to burst out of me—I held on to the key in my pocket for luck, still missing my beloved keychain, and I told my best friend.

> Ash,
>
> You will never guess what just happened to me!!!

I wasn't typically an exclamation point girl, but this situation needed them. Lots of them.

> My perfect stepsister, Belén's extra-special snow-flake, has just hired me to make her a website fueled by rule-breaking and subversion. I have been waiting for the day Tilly decided to rebel against her mother, and miraculously, it has arrived. She apparently "discovered a passion" for contemporary dance and is ready to tell ballet to take a hike. She's been keeping it to herself all summer. Can you believe that?!?!? My jaw is still lying on the floor, where it's been since I found out. I wish you could have seen her face when I told her she'd actually hired me, not some faceless professional like she thought, and that her fate was now resting in her lowly stepsister's hands. Of course, I haven't told Belén about my business, so Tilly could tattle on me if she wanted to as well. But I have a feeling she won't.

Anywho, I had to tell you. Even if you're still ready to throw me to the wolves, I knew you'd get a kick out of this. And, if you're not too annoyed with me still, feel free to offer any advice, tactics, or strategies ... You know, whatever you can think of. We are in uncharted territory, my friend.

Yours in conspiracy,
Tate

I typed without thinking, without tiptoeing around the elephant that sat firmly between us. When I finished and read it back to myself, I smiled. The old me, the one who cracked snarky jokes and shared secrets with her best friend, was still there; a little damaged, but still there. I hoped Ash could see that, and that the old her, the one who liked conspiring and commiserating, was still there too. I ran my index finger over the teeth of my substitute house key again and smiled.

And, because I was feeling pretty good about myself, I dashed off a quick note to my dad. The weight of our last conversation was hanging around my neck, and my improved mood reminded me I had the power to take that weight away.

Hi Dad,

Just checking in. I feel bad about hanging up on you the other night. It wasn't my finest hour, but I'm working on it.

Things here are status quo. You were right about my doing a lot of good with my work this summer. Hope you are too. Can't wait till you're back.

Love,
Tatum

I was deliberately vague about which work I was talking about, but he wouldn't know the difference. He must not have been in meetings or doing site visits, because he wrote back in minutes.

> That means a lot, sweetheart. I'm glad to hear things are looking up. Counting the days till I see you again.

In my bones, no matter how annoyed or upset I was over how things went down this summer, I knew I was counting the days too. Counting the days off the color-coded calendar until "Ken—out of country" was gone, counting the days till September first, when my sentence would be over, and counting the days, however many they might be, until I heard from my best friend again.

Chapter 12

I had to remind myself to stop checking my email for a response from Ash. I knew sitting in my room was only making it worse, constantly refreshing the browser in between working. I did get a note that Emily loved the book cover. She'd promptly filled my Paypal account with the full amount I'd asked for, and told me to expect emails from some of her writer friends. I was still freaking out that someone was paying me for creating art, but I'd take it. Between Emily's fee, what Abby had given me for her logo, and the Sol Jam posters, I was close to the amount I needed to save for the fine. SK's site and Tilly's portfolio would push me over the edge, leaving what I hoped would be a nice chunk to use toward that coveted tablet.

In a fit of nervous—but oddly positive—energy, as nothing had come from SK, or Ashlyn, or anyone else, I slammed the lid shut and flounced down the stairs, stomping my foot on each step. Each loud thud I made was more satisfying than the next. A silly, childish grin was on my face by the time I made it to the basement, where Blanche sat on the floor, cross-legged, playing solitaire on the glass coffee table.

"Good afternoon, Tatum," she said sweetly, without looking up from her cards.

"Good afternoon," I said with a smile.

Blanche chuckled. "You're in a good mood today for a change. I'm glad to see it. I worry about you sometimes, Tatum."

My cheeks colored. "It's not been the best summer ever, exactly, but you already know that."

"I do know that. Speaking of, I was walking upstairs the other night and heard something. Arguing. It may have come from the kitchen, but I couldn't be sure."

I didn't know how to respond. Did she want me to elaborate? She didn't say anything else, just turned the cards slowly, one by one, arranging them in their straight columns. The grin that had graced my face on the way down to the basement slid off and fell to the carpet at my feet. I dropped to the floor next to Blanche. "I snuck out the other night. I got caught."

"Probably not the wisest decision you've ever made." She turned another card.

"No, probably not. But, in my defense, that's the most disobedient thing I've done in my life. She thinks I'm always screwing up." We both knew which she I meant. "The thing I choose is always wrong, in her opinion."

"Our experiences inform our behaviors, Tatum. My

daughter's actions may not always be justified in your eyes, but I can understand where she's coming from."

"Do *you* think they're justified?" I asked. Comparing the differences between Blanche and Belén, it was easy to forget that Blanche was the one who'd made the rules and enforced them for so many years. "I mean, you're nothing alike. Sometimes, I have a hard time believing you're her mother."

Blanche chuckled softly. "I'm not sure my daughter would have ever followed my lead when it comes to parenting. Though the fact she asked me to come this summer warms my heart."

"She never asked for your help with Tilly?"

"When Matilda was born, we lived in different cities, and Belén was in law school as a very young widow. She relied on her friends as her support network, mostly."

"That makes no sense. You're awesome. Abuela of the Century."

Blanche laid the cards in her hand down on the table gently and faced me. "She hasn't had the easiest time, you know. Let me tell you a story, Tatum. It may help you understand. When we first moved from Chile for my husband's new job, she was still Belén. After the first week in her new elementary school, she begged to be called Brenda and put away the books she always carried. She didn't want to be different, any more than she already was. There were only a handful of other minority children in her school at the time, even fewer who weren't born here. The other children were interested in sports or playing princess, and she was not. She felt like she stuck

out. Also, many students were not very tactful, shall we
say. My little girl was called many names, some of them
cruel. I'm sure you know the inaccurate stereotypes that
exist. They looked down on her and she cried many tears,
just as you have."

A pang of regret hit me, but I stubbornly shook it off.
"Everyone's cried about something like that. I get it, but
I don't think that means she has to be so hard on me." I
crossed my arms and looked down at the floor.

Blanche picked up the cards again and began turning the ones in her stack. "She did what she thought was
right. She still does."

I rephrased my earlier question. "Do you think the
way she's treated me is right?"

She ignored me and started placing the twos and
threes on the aces. "In hindsight, I can see her father and
I were just as overwhelmed by our new life as she was,
grasping at straws. We did everything we thought might
help her adjust. We took American names ourselves at
the suggestion of some immigrant friends. We watched
American television. We even let her try out for cheerleading, twice, like the other girls down the street did,
though she never made the team." I guessed Belén was
now living vicariously through Tilly's accomplishments.
"She avoided the more academic endeavors I know she
would have excelled at because she saw those activities as
undesirable."

I could picture that, and it made me sad for her. And
also sad that she thought doing something she probably
didn't like would help her fit in. Cheerleading was so not

part of Belén's personality. Too bad she hadn't stumbled across Debate.

"She didn't really get close to anyone until she was in college," said Blanche.

"So she never had a best girlfriend in high school?"

"She did not. She avoided anything that wasn't required, because she didn't feel she belonged. Her father and I eventually decided to just let her be, for fear she would become further withdrawn if we pressed more."

Sympathy winged through me again. No one deserved that. My breath caught in my throat, as I tried to think of an adequate response. Luckily, Blanche kept going, and I stayed quiet.

"Belén wanted to be blonde and popular like the prom queens and the class presidents, but when she looked in the mirror, she saw her serious face, and her dark hair and skin. It is devastating to know your peers make assumptions about you based on what you look like, where you come from, and your interests. She desperately wanted to feel that she was good enough. That she could be special and important too. Yet, because of the actions of others, she convinced herself that she could never amount to anything."

My snark antenna went up at that, and I clenched my jaw. "But that's exactly what it feels like she does to me. I don't understand."

Blanche ignored my sassiness again and kept on turning cards and telling her tale. "Her father and I feared she'd never find peace with herself. But when she got to college, everything changed. Her very first class was

taught by a highly intelligent and successful woman with
a doctorate degree. Belén was completely starstruck and
inspired. The professor was everything Belén dreamed
of being, and she wasn't blonde. It was almost as if this
woman gave her permission to be Belén again. She also
introduced her to other like-minded students and profes-
sors on campus. People from all backgrounds. For the first
time, she had friends. They accepted her just as she was,
and her confidence began to return." There was a wistful-
ness to Blanche's voice as she spoke that hadn't been there
before.

"Wasn't that a good thing?"

"Of course. I was happy for my little girl. She earned
prestigious internships and was invited to conferences and
even on vacations with her new friends. But she came
home less and less. In some ways, her group became an
alternate family."

I looked at Blanche and saw the lines of heartache
in her face. "Do you regret it? Not pushing her harder?
I mean, do you think she looks back on her childhood
and wishes she'd been a ballerina and a pianist and taken
a million honors classes, like she made Tilly do? Do you
think she believes that would have been better? I mean,
that ludicrous parenting blog she loves probably makes her
feel like she missed out."

She looked directly into my eyes, with a renewed
intensity. "I will never regret doing what I thought was
right for my child. Even if, looking back, she wishes I had
chosen differently for her. And I would wager that Belén
feels the same way now about Matilda. And you."

"So, then what? She met these people, found herself, found validation, and ...?"

Blanche sighed. "She met Matilda's father through her college friends, she graduated, they got married, she became pregnant right away. Daniel died unexpectedly during the pregnancy, and a few years later, she met your father. You know the rest."

"So she learned how to be a dictator from her college and law school friends?"

Blanche looked at me sharply. "I don't think that's a fair assessment, Tatum."

My face fell. She'd never chastised me before. "Sorry."

"And no, I don't think that. I will always be grateful to her college friends for bringing her back to herself and supporting her when she needed it. However, I do think that becoming a parent changed her view on a lot of things. You'll probably feel the same one day. The way she has chosen to raise Matilda certainly suggests she believes setting a particular type of example is better than others. Whether it came from her friends, the internet, books, out of spite for me, I do not know. She and I do not always agree on what happiness or success look like; but we do wish for the same things, regardless of definition, for Matilda, and for you."

I would've thought this would be the point where Blanche became angry or upset about Belén's choices, but she went back to matter-of-fact. Maybe I'd been wrong about her? I raised one eyebrow. "And she'd probably flip her lid if I said I wanted to be a cheerleader. Does she think she's protecting us?"

"Some things are hard to forget, Tatum. Do not underestimate the power fear has over our choices." Blanche shifted the cards in her hands back and forth, as if trying to decide if she wanted to play another game or not. "As I said, we do what we think is right for our children. I did, and she does."

I had a hard time imagining Belén being afraid of anything. Her tough exterior, in my eyes, had always made her the thing to be feared. And yet, on the other hand, it all made sense.

"If your choices back then were so wrong"—I made bunny ears—"how come you kept the name Blanche?"

She smiled faintly. "When you find something you love, something that suits you, you stick with it."

I nodded. "So, not to be dense, but what was the point of this story?"

She laid the cards back down on the table in a neat pile. "I wanted you to have some context, Tatum. It's just an explanation."

"For why she's been so hard on me?"

"If that's how you'd like to see it. I was actually hoping it might encourage you to examine your own actions."

Oh. I flushed again, but this time with shame. Had I really been so awful to Belén? "Right. Um, thanks for sharing." Dazed, I climbed the stairs and went back to my room.

I wanted to empathize with my stepmother, even though I'd never really been able to before. I was glad Blanche told me what growing up was like in their house, though. I couldn't even imagine what it would have felt like to be teased or judged for the way I looked. I kinda wanted to go back in time and dropkick those kids for being ignorant jerks. Blonde was fine, but it wasn't equal to perfection, and Belén was prettier and smarter than almost anyone else—her strictness couldn't take that away. I knew Blanche was trying to get me to stop being so stubborn, and I guess deep down I agreed with her. Even I could brush away my righteous indignation to see it was possible that all of Belén's rules for life came from a place of good intentions. Care for me and a desire to protect me. But changing the way I responded to her rules? Actually doing it would be harder than thinking about it. Unraveling years of feeling hurt and overlooked was going to take a lot of effort on my part. Then again, if Blanche and Belén could build a bridge, maybe Belén and I could as well. If I wanted to make even a ripple in this pond, I was going to have to be the bigger person. I just hoped I had the strength to do it.

Chapter 13

Dear Tate,

Seriously? I can't believe it. I always knew there was more underneath the surface with Tilly than she let on.

I kind of have to give her props, though, for going behind the stepmonster's back. Belén is going to freak when she finds out. Wouldn't it be terrific if your dad and Belén came for the end-of-summer performance and, oops, no one's wearing toe shoes?

You have to make the site for her, no question. Make it really gorgeous, make her look like the greatest dancer in the world so she gets a scholarship, and then there's no way of keeping that secret.

Unbelievable.

Ash

When I read Ashlyn's response, without pretentious adjectives and lawyer-ese, my heart started fluttering. She hadn't mentioned our fight, my supposed betrayal, her forced departure from Henderson High School society, or any of the still-lingering tensions that spanned the miles that lay between us. A tiny balloon of hope began to inflate inside of me. I was afraid of that hope, of being disappointed, so I didn't encourage it. Much. I did flinch at her use of my old favorite term, *stepmonster*. Maybe Blanche's words of wisdom were sinking in. A little.

> Ash,
>
> I know, right?!? I'm definitely making the site, and I sure as heck am charging her. No family discount for the swan princess. Guess I'll need another nickname for her now, though.
>
> In other news, I'm beginning to look like the Hunchback of Notre Dame from all the bending over as I cut down scary plants. Remind me not to do this next year.
>
> Love,
> Tate

I hit *send* before I realized what I'd written. A bolt of paranoia struck me the minute the email left the screen, and I pulled it up again from my "sent mail" box. I'd signed off with "love."

I was scared that one word, a word that carried so much weight, would take us back two steps when we'd finally gone forward one. It also occurred to me, as I reread my impulsive words, that asking her to remind me not to do this again could be interpreted many ways, and what if she took it wrong? My heart sped up anxiously. Would she think I meant I didn't want to pull plants again, or deal with a grand larceny charge again? Not that I wanted to do either ever again, but I didn't want her to read too much into it. I blinked at the screen before shutting the lid and going to the closet to change. Maybe what I was actually saying to her was that I didn't want to fight with her again. In truth, fighting was the thing I wanted least of all.

As much as I had complained about the way my clothes were always soaked through after a shift, and how I'd probably be wearing a back brace for the first semester of junior year, I knew I would miss my time on the Invasive Plant Removal Team. The friendships I'd forged with Abby and Hunter made every ache, pain, and trail of sweat just a little more bearable. It was nice to suffer—in regard to the plants and the oppressive house rules—with others, as Blanche had rightly alluded to after my first day.

The afternoon we finished with the ivy, I looked up at the bare trees, hands on my hips, and smiled.

"We did good, kids," Abby said, also admiring our work.

I nodded. "Right? I feel like maybe we did something worthwhile this summer. Even though it sucked most of the time."

Hunter took off his gloves and wiped the sweat off his brow. "Sucked doesn't even cover it. But you're right. I'm glad we did this together." Abby grinned at him. "And it also doesn't hurt that my biceps look amazing. I may have to wear a sleeveless shirt for Sol Jam to show off these guns." He flexed dramatically for us, and Abby and I dutifully pretended to be groupies, drooling over the big-deal musician.

"You must work out for *hours*," Abby fawned, and petted Hunter's arm. I batted my eyelashes at him.

"It's important to look good for my fans. Give them what they want," he said in a fake pompous voice.

I rolled my eyes and stood up straighter. Alicia was approaching to inspect our section, making sure we hadn't missed anything.

"Speaking of Sol Jam, how's interest looking?" I asked. According to Abby, Kyle had approached the property owner about selling tickets this year. Owen didn't want to charge, said "music should be free," but he agreed that tickets were a good way to get an estimate of how many people might be coming. I'd created a ticket that matched the poster—the one Paolo liked, now modified to include all the participating bands—which currently hung in the window of most of Northern Virginia's coffee shops and on community event bulletin boards. I was ridiculously proud of that.

"Kyle says it looks like we've already passed last year's attendance, so it's definitely looking good. He's betting over two hundred people will show up."

I raised both eyebrows. "That many?"

Hunter puffed his chest up. "I told you we were popular." He deflated and laughed at himself.

"As you should be," Abby declared. "We should probably make a plan for that day, Tatum."

A plan. I'd been so wrapped up in the drama at home that I'd just sort of assumed I'd be staying in while everyone else was at Sol Jam. A good-faith effort on my part to follow the rules. And I'd forgotten to mention that part to Abby, who still thought I was going to be her right hand for article coverage. If I was going to make a valiant attempt at putting myself in Belén's shoes, I needed to actually stay put.

"Well," I started, but Alicia cut me off. She'd finished checking our area, and seemed pleased, judging by the easy smile on her face.

"Amazing work, guys. I don't see any ivy left. The park service is really going to be happy to see this."

"Thanks, Alicia." She high-fived me and offered fist bumps to Abby and Hunter.

"Who needs their hours verified? You, right, Tatum?"

I looked down at the ground and drew a circle in the dirt with my toe. "Yep."

"Oh, me too, Alicia. My probation officer will be so thrilled to see that signature." Alicia looked at Abby quizzically, and then shrugged it off as Abby just smiled.

"Sure, just bring the paperwork to the office before you leave for the day."

"You got it." Abby gave her a cheesy thumbs-up as Alicia walked toward another group.

"Why did you say that?" I whispered.

"I didn't want her to think you were the only one

who got dealt a bad hand." Abby put an arm around my sticky shoulders. "That's what friends do, T."

All the blood in my head rushed to my ears, and tears stung the corners of my eyes. "Thanks."

"You're good people, Tatum," she said, and tightened her grip on me.

I looked down at the ground again, overcome, and saw Hunter take Abby's other hand and squeeze as he said, "You both are."

> Hi Tate,
>
> Sorry it's been so long. We just got home. I'm not sure how to respond to your last email. I'm glad you liked my music? No one's ever said I wrecked them, so I hope that's a good thing. Are you okay now? Do I need to send the paramedics or a construction crew to repair you? All joking aside, I don't think I've ever gotten a nicer compliment. As corny as it sounds, I think music is meant to touch your soul and bring out emotions you didn't know were there. It does for me, anyway. Don't tell anyone I said that. Maybe you should delete this email after you read it. Or burn your computer, whatever's easier.

I laughed. I was definitely keeping the email. If SK ever became famous, toured the world, and won Grammy awards, I could pull this email out as proof that he'd once been just like the rest of us.

How's the site coming, by the way? Anything I
can see yet?

SK

I'd been working steadily on SK's portfolio site, adding the audio clips that he'd sent me, careful not to click on
them as I worked in an act of self-preservation. There'd been
enough tears already. SK's cello résumé was ridiculously
impressive and filled with years of performances, awards, and
private lessons. As I was formatting it for the site, my mind
couldn't help but stray to the list of accomplishments I'd had
to submit when I'd applied to McIntosh two years ago. A lot
of good it had done me then, all those years of art lessons and
design tutorials. I had to remind myself that even though
they'd rejected me, I was still able to use my skills with
TLC. A little voice in the back of my mind kept nagging me
that I could also use them to get into college too. I hoped.

I attached a mock-up of the site to an open email, fingers
crossed that he'd like what he saw. I'd made a point to design
the site in shades of brown, per his wacky favorite color,
and added, in a moment of whimsy, a stylized version of the
photograph he'd sent me from Ireland as part of the header
across the top of the main page. I'd changed it to sepia tones
and made the grass a vibrant green, the only other color on
the page. It wasn't flashy, but it felt like the perfect combination of dedicated, relaxed, and fun, just like him.

Hi SK,

Glad you made it home safely. Here's the site so
far; it's almost done. Let me know what you think
and if you want any adjustments made. The one

thing that's missing is a photograph of you, if you're cool with that. Got any you'd like to use?

I wouldn't use the word corny. I'd say sensitive. Maybe delicate. Touchy-feely?

Emotionally yours,
Tate

Did I really just send an email to a boy with "yours" in the valediction? I put both elbows on my desk and squished my cheeks between my hands. I hoped he didn't read too much into that and think I was overstepping the boundaries of a professional relationship. I snorted at the thought. We'd already crossed that line, right? Maybe I did hope he'd read more into it.

Tate—love the Ireland pic! Genius. My mom will be so chuffed to see that. (Did you catch my across-the-pond language there?) You get bonus points for the brown. Clearly, you pay attention to details—I like that in a girl.

Alas, the only "professional" photos I have are the headshots from my application to McIntosh, and they'll never see the light of day. I'll just leave you with one word—braces. I have some performances coming up soon, though, so I'll try and get you some action shots. Do you think those will be okay?

Enthusiastically Yours,
SK

I read with wide eyes, unbelieving. We were definitely over the line. He liked that in a girl? My pulse quickened a little as I allowed myself a moment of imagination, wondering what we might think of each other if we met in person. What if I asked him if I could come to one of these performances—you know, for research? What if he said no? That would be embarrassing. What if he said yes and we met and had a completely awkward moment where neither of us said anything, and we stood around looking at the floor? Better to just stick to words.

SK—yes, can't wait to see them!

Break a leg,
Tate

But ten seconds later, I realized I didn't want to wait for him to send the photographs. Wondering why I hadn't done it earlier, I typed his full name into my browser and pressed *search*. The results included three years' worth of concert programs from McIntosh, and press releases for the awards I already knew about from his résumé. Bingo. His accolades were interspersed with a handful of links to social media sites; I clicked on the one at the top, hoping to see a friendly smile that matched SK's sense of humor, and held my breath. When his profile revealed nothing more than a very nice picture of a cello, I exhaled. Bust. The second and third sites were the same. I had to give SK credit for his skills in the area of internet privacy, but I was also a little crushed. My efforts thwarted, I reminded myself that the best things were worth waiting for. And, somehow, I knew that finally seeing SK's face would be worth it. I could wait.

Chapter 14

The completed survey for Tilly's website was sitting on my bed when I returned from the shower, wrapped in a towel. I stood over it and peered down, a droplet of water falling from my dripping hair onto the paper. No surprise, it was written in Tilly's tiny, neat, and perfectly formed handwriting. It was so uniform, it could have been its own font. I was "babysitting" that night, so I tossed the papers in my satchel with my laptop for later.

As I pulled out a T-shirt from the middle dresser drawer, an idea hit me. Why not take Tilly with me? If she agreed, it could be a useful evening in more ways than one. We could work on her site together, and I could make sure she didn't have any plans to spill my secret. I smiled to myself as I rubbed the towel over my wet hair and threw on my clothes.

Like we'd planned it, Tilly and I opened our bedroom doors and stepped into the hallway at the exact same time.

I sprang. "So, I'm going to ask you something at breakfast."

"Why don't you just ask me now?"

"Too much to explain. But I need you to trust me. I realize you have no reason to, but I'm asking you to try. Just play along, okay?"

Visibly confused, but too polite to argue with me, Tilly nodded, and we went downstairs.

At the breakfast table, Blanche sat next to Tilly, both of them sipping from mugs displaying names of universities Tilly was considering. Belén stood at the counter as I took my faithful Georgetown mug from the cabinet and filled it with hot water from the kettle. Blanche patted the place mat at the seat next to her, where a peppermint tea bag lay waiting for me. I flashed her a grateful grin, and she smiled back, her expression feeling like sunlight in an otherwise arctic room. Tilly eyed me over the rim of her Swarthmore mug, looking scared. I winked at her and sat down.

"So, Tilly, are we still on for tonight? You'll be home in time, right?"

I noticed the grip on her mug got tighter. Belén looked up, brows furrowed and mouth in a frown. I'm sure if I were her, I would have done the same, hearing that Tilly and I had plans for the first time in, well, ever.

"What's going on tonight?"

I casually sipped my tea. "Tilly is coming to the Schmidts' with me so we can work on a project together." When Belén wasn't looking at me, I mouthed *trust me* at Tilly, and her deer-in-headlights expression softened slightly.

Belén crossed and stood at the head of the table, towering over the three of us. "What kind of project, Matilda?"

Tilly sank in her seat a little bit and took a deep breath. "Tatum, why don't you tell her?"

I smiled beatifically at my stepmother. "Well, Tilly was interested in making an online portfolio for college, and she asked me to help her. It seems to be something admissions panels might like, especially if it shows videos of her dancing."

Tilly nodded her head furiously, catching on. "That's right, Mama. The colleges we've been considering all require an art supplement in addition to an audition, so I thought this would be a creative way to do it. It would make me unique from the other applicants." Nicely played, stepsister.

It was like watching the numbers on a slot machine line up. Belén's face went from confused, to contemplative, and finally to accepting in a matter of seconds. She nodded slowly, like she was letting the idea of Tilly and me working together for a cause she actually supported marinate, sink down in the recesses of her mind until it popped back up on the surface. "That sounds very productive."

Huh. I'd expected at least a little protest, especially since it was me doing the helping, but even Belén couldn't deny that I had at least the basic skills. When I got rejected from MacIntosh, she'd acted like the outcome reflected poorly on her personally for some reason. She was weird like that. And then a lightning bolt rammed itself into my brain. What if she remembered my portfolio positively, and her annoyance at the rejection wasn't directed at *me*, but the admissions peeps? Had I been looking at her behavior from the wrong angle this whole time? The idea that Belén was putting me first, in her own sometimes misguided way, was blowing my mind a little.

"Yes, it should be. We'll get started once the girls go to bed," I said, and smiled again, a real one this time.

Blanche looked from me to Tilly, to Belén, and then back to me. "What a wonderful sisterly endeavor, Tatum. You both are so busy, it's no surprise you never get any quality time together." Like that was the reason. Blanche turned her eyes to her daughter and grinned, full and wide, like she was trying to convince her. "Isn't it wonderful, mi hija? Both of these talented young women working as a team."

Belén nodded again and turned to Tilly, a slight smile playing on her lips. "You will show this to me before we send any applications." Like they were applying as a team. Would it be Team Tatum when I applied to college too?

"Of course, Mama."

Tilly and Belén finished their tea, then disappeared into the garage on their way out for the day—Belén to work and Tilly to rehearsal. I stayed at the table, pleased with my handiwork, slowly sipping my drink and thinking about making something with a higher caloric content for breakfast when Blanche poked me in the shoulder.

"What are you up to?"

I widened my eyes with feigned innocence. "What do you mean?"

"That's the first conversation I've seen you and Matilda have since I've been here."

"I'm not allowed to talk to my stepsister?" I winked at her and took my empty tea cup to the sink.

"Of course you are. But I don't believe for a second that you and Matilda made a plan ahead of time."

I took two waffles from the freezer and popped them into the toaster. "That's because we didn't. But you aren't the one who needed to believe it."

"Is there really a website?"

"Yep. Well, there will be after I build it."

"And is Matilda planning to use it in her applications?"

"She sure is."

The toaster ejected my waffles and I put them on a plate. I turned back to Blanche, whose eyes were narrowed, but she was smiling as if to say that my explanation was good enough for her. I smiled angelically and took my waffles upstairs.

After Tilly got home from dance and showered—thank goodness, because dancing hard equals sweating buckets—I hustled her into the car.

"Have fun, girls," Belén called after us. I almost tripped on her enthusiasm and pleasant tone.

"We will," I called back. It was odd to exchange these little nicey-nice words with her. But I couldn't say I didn't like it, and that was odd too.

"She's in a good mood," I said to Tilly as we took off down the street, realizing that Belén had failed, for the first time, to check the mileage on my car. Blanche's voice whispered in my ear about being more pleasant to Belén. Maybe there was something to that.

Tilly didn't respond, but I noticed the corners of her mouth lift slightly. I took that as a good sign. When I opened the door to the Schmidt house, Tilly looked around, clearly puzzled by the emptiness.

"Where is everyone? Aren't you supposed to be watching Maya and Kate?"

At the sound of her voice, Gus darted out of the kitchen toward us and wound himself around my ankles.

I started up the stairs, a confused Tilly following me cautiously, Gus prancing right behind her. "Yeah, about that. Maya and Kate are actually on an extended vacation with their parents." I didn't turn around to check, but I knew she must be shocked. I could feel it radiating off of her.

"And when you say extended vacation, does that mean this week? The last two weeks?"

At the top of the stairs, I turned and faced her with a smirk. "The whole summer, actually."

Tilly's expression floored me. Not only was she not judging me, she looked daunted and in awe. "You've been lying the whole time?"

I stood directly in front of her, hip cocked, hand on the wall. "I told you I could keep a secret."

"But why?"

"What would you have done if you were me? In one fell swoop, I lost my dad, I lost my friend, and I lost what shaky trust I had from your mom and probably you too." Her face colored. "I've been confined to my room and to manual labor for weeks now. And to top it off, it feels like there's no one on my side."

She looked away, embarrassed, and I sighed.

"I didn't really expect you to come to my rescue, Tilly, so stop feeling guilty. But can you see why I would keep this for myself? And, technically, I didn't completely lie." I led Tilly into Kate's room, where Mr. Blue swam lazily toward us from the confines of his little glass bowl.

She let out a very unladylike and thus un-Tilly-like snort. "You've been fish sitting?"

I sprinkled some flakes on top of the water. "And cat and hamster sitting too. Princess Sweetheart is very unpredictable. She might rob a bank if no one is looking. Or commit grand larceny." I raised an eyebrow at her, and she looked away again.

We moved to Maya's room. I busied myself with changing the hamster's water and food while Tilly sat primly on the bed and stared at the wall. I wondered how she wasn't sore all over from holding her back so straight and mashing her knees together, bent at perfect right angles.

Upstairs pets taken care of, I headed toward the door to feed Gus and set up shop downstairs. "Come on," I called to Tilly, who plodded behind me like I was leading her to the guillotine. She hovered nearby while I scooped the cat food into Gus's silver bowl.

"You could pretend to be happy about spending time with me." Job done, I led her into the living room, sat on my favorite couch, and pulled my laptop from my bag. "Sit down, you won't regret it."

Tilly perched gingerly on the edge and the cushions

gave way to her slight weight, sending her sprawling backward, legs full-on in the air. Laughter erupted from me, spilling over the both of us, so engulfing that Tilly started giggling too. When we'd both calmed down enough to speak, I was overwhelmed with a sudden sadness.

"I can't remember the last time I heard you laugh," I said quietly.

Tilly's mouth formed a horizontal line. "Me either."

I smiled. "Maybe you need to come over and sit on this couch with me more often."

"Maybe so." She smiled back. "All right, about this portfolio. We're clear that it needs to be contemporary, right? I felt like you were siding with my mom this morning, and were going to make one for classical ballet to be mean."

"No way. That was just A, to buy us time to work on it here and, B, so you can prepare yourself to tell her you don't want to wear tutus anymore."

"I hate tutus with a passion, Tatum. You have no idea."

I shook my head, amazed. The things Tilly had kept to herself.

"Oh, I think I definitely do." We both laughed again, which felt unbelievably good and like something between us shifted into place.

Being the overachieving planner that she was, Tilly had given me access to her online storage drive packed full of photographs and videos of her dancing this summer. She played a few of her favorites for me, and it took me back to watching the girl on TV who had captivated

me so much. But my stepsister was surprisingly more talented at it. The clip I liked the best showed Tilly dancing
erratically to an old Nirvana song, of all things, and the
angst on her face was terrifying. I totally related.

"This is unbelievable. Your mom will die when she
sees this."

She raised one eyebrow. "Maybe just a small stroke."

"Was that a joke you made, Matilda? About your
sainted mother, no less?"

She giggled. "Possibly."

I pulled up a template I'd created for the basis for SK's
site, and quickly added Tilly's photos and uploaded her
résumé, now complete with contemporary experience.
We could make it pretty later. "Don't you want to add in
some ballet stuff too? That's the bulk of your experience."

"I guess you're right." She picked out the most beautiful shots, showcasing her technique and strength, and a
video of her dancing the role of the Sugar Plum Fairy last
Christmas.

Bolstered by our tentative joking and perhaps my will-
ingness to help her pull one over on her mom, Tilly became
bolder as we neared the end of our evening together.

"Do you miss her?" she asked as we worked.

"Who?"

She sank deep into the couch, dwarfed by the pillows.
"Ashlyn."

Oh. She wanted to go there. "Actually, yes, I do
miss her."

She sighed, the sound muffled by all the canvas and
fluff. "I was always jealous of you guys."

"What? Did I hear that right? You jealous of me?" I stuck a finger to my ear and pretended to clean out imaginary wax. There was no way she just said that.

"Yes, you heard me correctly. You guys were two peas in a pod. I've never had a friend like that. Do you remember Ashlyn's dad's party that one Christmas?"

"The one where your mom blew everything out of proportion?

"She thought you were drinking. Do you blame her?" I raised a finger into the air. "But there was no actual drinking. None at all. And she still went ballistic."

Mr. Zanotti had thrown a ginormous holiday party for his friends and clients the December we started high school. Ash had brought four champagne flutes filled with ginger ale into her bedroom, where she and I had been hiding out. She downed her two drinks in minutes, while I nursed one as we turned Ash's music up loud and sang even louder. Halfway through my amazing rendition of "I Will Survive," while using my half-filled glass as a microphone, Belén walked in. She startled me so much, I jumped and spilled the contents of my glass down my front. All Belén saw were three empty glasses, the "champagne" staining my new dress, and the fourth glass sitting bubbling on Ash's dresser. She grabbed my elbow, marched me right out the front door, and gave me a lecture about making responsible choices.

"Your mom was really mad. Even though I told her up and down that there was no booze anywhere near me, and told her I knew better, she said even pretending was dangerous. She took my phone away for a month. Told me I was going to activate the alcoholic gene or something." Belén rarely ignored an opportunity to remind me of my mother's indiscretions. I was glad I could laugh about it months and months later. I'd been offended at the time, though.

Tilly looked down at her hands in her lap. "She was so upset. I overheard her crying about it to your dad after we got home. She was really afraid for you, I think."

My heart stopped, and my mouth went completely dry. Belén had cried about me? It certainly fit with all the facts I'd been gathering about her this summer, about her desire for me to be safe and responsible, but hearing Tilly acknowledge that her mother felt genuine affection for me was hard to process. I had obviously been the one who hadn't been paying attention.

Tilly saved me from needing to form a coherent response and continued. "I was glad she was mad at you, because I was mad too."

"Why?"

"Because you and Ash didn't invite me to join you." Oh. Definitely hadn't been paying attention. At all. "You always seem to have so much fun, and I don't really have time for friends. I would have gladly taken any consequence my mom laid out to be part of that."

"I'm so sorry, Tilly. I never realized." She shrugged, like it wasn't a big deal, but I knew it was. "Aren't you tight with the other bunheads?"

"No. It's all competition with them. You rarely get a compliment that's not backhanded. They're so wrapped up in themselves that there isn't time to make friends."

"I've heard that said about some artists before, actually." The conversation with the random hot guy the night of Tilly's showcase fluttered in my mind. That seemed like so very long ago. Tilly's isolation sounded not too far off from what Belén had dealt with growing up as well. I wondered if she knew about her mom's experiences.

"Yes, we're all messes. You included." She peeked out from the pillows and grinned at me.

"You think I'm an artist?" I lowered my eyes and glanced at her from beneath my lashes.

"Are you kidding?" Her voice rose. "This is amazing. I could never design anything. I'm computer deficient. I'm lucky I can send an email."

"You have, in fact, successfully sent at least one email. I can prove that." Our laughter finally felt easy. The paralyzing tension that had existed between us for years, an invisible barrier of jealousy and assumptions that had pushed us farther and farther away from each other, had finally started to dissipate.

As if she noticed the calm in the room at the same time I did, Tilly looked at me again and offered another smile. One that looked like the kind Abby wore and the kind I hoped I'd see again from Ashlyn. I smiled back and offered her my hand.

"Truce?"

She shook it firmly, and this time I wasn't caught off guard by her strength. "Truce."

"Great. Because I think I'm going to need your help with something."

"You helped me." Tilly smiled. "What can I do?"

"I need to get out of the house, and I think it will be easier, and more fun, if you come with me. There will be amazing music involved." Tilly raised an eyebrow. "Trust me, you'll love it."

Dear Tate,

Please send pictures of you as the hunchback. I'd like that for my new locker, please.

How's it going with Tilly? Has she told Belén yet? Have you?

So my roommate lives in The Plains, and was telling me about this music thing there next weekend. I thought if you could get away, maybe we could meet up there? She's giving me a ride, and I won't know anyone else going. No big deal if you can't. Just thought I'd check.

I miss you,
Ash

The holy grail of best friend valedictions had just landed in my inbox. I wanted to weep with joy, if I did that sort of thing, or jump up and down on my bed with happiness.

Over the course of my summer of imprisonment, I'd decided something: Ash hadn't done anything wrong either. Sure, she'd gotten in way too deep with a criminal, but I was willing to forgive her. I believed her when she said she didn't know Chase was going to steal. I believed she didn't intend to involve me. Once the emotions had faded and I was left with facts, I realized our long, solid friendship was all the proof I needed. I was sure we both would be able to let it go and move on. But before that part could happen, we'd need to talk. Really talk. The last time we'd spoken in person was in the police car, and two months was a long time to let hurt fester. The talking probably wouldn't be pretty, but I'd learned a lot about myself this summer. I knew I would be okay, no matter what Ash said back to me.

I'd already planned to find a way to get to Sol Jam, but now? Of course I would find a way to meet her. I had a lot to tell my best friend.

I'll be there.

I miss you too,
Tate

Chapter 15

When I'd brought up going to Sol Jam to Tilly, she'd been wary.

"I don't lie, Tatum. She'll know."

"Oh, please." Her eyes widened at my brashness. "You've been lying to her for months."

I told her about working on the article about the Frisson with Abby, and how I wanted to be there for the last hurrah before she put the article together. "I only made it to one band practice and Abby's been to a lot now. This could be really great for my business too."

Tilly, thankfully, understood where I was coming from, though we both agreed that we didn't want to lie anymore. We spent the next several days trying to think of a way to persuade Belén that the concert was a good idea. I even wrote up a list of reasons she should give her permission: I'd be supporting local artists and therefore bettering our community; I would have a great experience to start off my no-doubt illustrious career with the school paper; Tilly would be there to make sure I followed any and all rules for the outing; etc. When I read the list back to myself, though, I wasn't convinced my reasons would be good enough, and lost my nerve.

As it turned out, neither of us needed to have worried. The morning before the concert, Belén pulled out a burgundy marker—her assigned color—and wrote "Belén—work trip" across Friday, Saturday, and Sunday on the family calendar.

"I have a last-minute conference in Philadelphia this weekend," she announced, as Tilly and I eyed each other over plates of scrambled eggs. "One of the other partners at the firm is having emergency surgery, so I need to step in and present."

"That sounds like a nice change of pace, Mama," Tilly said brightly.

Belén poured coffee into a silver travel mug. "It's more annoying than anything, having to shift gears, but I suppose it will be nice to get out of the office for a little while. Now, while I'm gone, obviously, my mother will be in charge. The rules remain the same." She turned her gaze to me as if to make a point. "And, because I won't be able to do it myself, I expect the weekend chores to be completed in my absence." Who did she want to do them? Me? Tilly? Blanche? All of us? "Tatum, I'll leave you a list."

Just me. I should have figured. Perhaps I could use this to my advantage. "If I get everything done, would you be okay if Tilly and I went out for a little while? We would give Blanche the mileage and take our phones and check in when we're on our way back." I pleaded with my eyes and hoped she would reconsider her ban on fun, just for this one night.

"Please, Mama," Tilly added. "I think we both deserve a little time off from all our hard work."

Belén checked her watch. It was time for her to leave for the office. I knew from years of observing her hurrying out the door that if she waited long enough to think about a valid reason to deny our request, she would get stuck in the Northern Virginia traffic that was almost as oppressive as the heat. She chose the lesser of the two evils. "Fine. But make sure you tell my mother all the important details, and if she has any reservations, she can veto the plan. Understood?"

"Understood," I said quickly, so she wouldn't change her mind.

"And only if the chores are done," Belén called over her shoulder. "Have a nice weekend, girls." Hearing my stepmother wish us goodbye collectively for the second time in recent days was still unnerving. But I could definitely get used to it.

I saluted the door as it closed behind her. When I heard the dull thud of the garage door closing and the hum of Belén's car engine fade into the distance, I whooped out loud. Victory!

"Does that freak you out when she says that?" I asked Tilly. "Calling us 'girls,' I mean."

Tilly laughed softly. "A little bit. We've never really been that. Until now, that is."

I whooped again. Two victories.

I waited until the episode of *The Golden Girls* Blanche was watching had ended before dumping our plan to go to Sol Jam on her. She listened patiently to my heartfelt plea for her cooperation.

"Tatum, I'm not sure about this."

"Belén actually did give us permission to go out. She just didn't know what I had in mind." I listed for Blanche the same reasons we should go that I'd given Tilly. "It's better this way. Bonus, I've now told a trusted adult where I'm going just in case something should go wrong."

She nodded slowly. By the lines in her forehead, I could see how hard it was for her to choose between Belén and me. "I have one condition."

"What's that?" I was ready to agree to anything if she was willing to give us the green light.

"You talk things out with your father when he gets home next week. Tell him, and Belén, how you've been feeling. Show them the work you've completed and your plans to do more."

I knew she was going to say that. And even I could admit it was a good idea, in theory, but in practice? "I see what you're trying to do here, and I appreciate the thought, but it might not do any good. I'm pretty sure they've already made up their mind about me."

Blanche gave me a look that was unmistakably an effort to make me see how stubborn I was being.

"Fine. I'll try."

"Nothing is immovable, Tatum. Everything is negotiable."

I smirked and nodded at the TV. "Did you learn that from *The Golden Girls?*"

She smiled back. "It might have been *The Facts of Life.*"

The morning of Sol Jam, I got up early to make sure I had all the chores on my list completed in time to get cleaned up before we hit the road.

The list, written on Belén's signature stationary, read:

- *Clean all bathrooms*
- *Vacuum all carpeted floors*
- *Sweep all hardwood floors*
- *Dust baseboards, crown moldings, and ceiling fans*

I gulped. This was going to take forever. I opened the cabinet under the sink and pulled out the caddy of cleaning supplies. Might as well start with the messiest part first and tackle the bathrooms. As I was pulling on the floppy yellow rubber gloves, Tilly knocked softly on the door frame.

"Morning."

"Good morning," I said, waving a gloved hand.

"Look at what I just found slipped under my door." Tilly held out a folded piece of paper.

> Matilda,
>
> A little magic for your adventure. Be good to each other.
>
> All My Love,
> Abuela

"What does she mean, magic?" I asked.

Tilly revealed an envelope in the hand she'd kept behind her back. "She left us a gift certificate for pedicures. And the spa happens to be on our way to the concert."

I'd never been to a spa before, never had a pedicure, never had my hair done other than the occasional trim. Belén hadn't been the kind of mother figure who told Tilly and me that we were beautiful inside and out, nor had she filled our heads with dreams of a fairy-tale ending. Now I understood why, but I was grateful for Blanche and her ways of making us feel special on a special night just the same.

"That was so sweet. She's the actual best," I murmured.

Tilly nodded. "I haven't spent enough time with her this summer. That definitely needs to change."

"Let's take her out to tea or something before she leaves," I suggested, pulling the toilet brush from the supply caddy. "Do you think we'll have enough time to go to the spa after I get all this cleaning done?" I wanted to make good on the deal and do what Belén had asked, but hanging out with Tilly and getting my toenails done sounded awfully tempting.

Tilly reached down and grabbed the feather duster from the caddy. "We will if I take half. How about you do the bathrooms and the vacuuming, and I'll take the dusting and the sweeping?"

"Really?" I felt my mouth pop open in surprise.

"Really."

My heart almost exploded into little pieces all over the tile floor. "Thank you," I said shyly.

"You would do the same for me," she replied, tapping me on the head with the duster. "Let's get a move on. And make sure it's spotless."

I stuck my tongue out at her. "You are so your mother's daughter."

Tilly just shrugged and did a chassé step out of the bathroom.

Buoyed by Tilly's selflessness and the growing anticipation of the event to come—or maybe it was the fumes from the disinfectant—my mood went from a five to a ten as I sprayed the mirror and buffed away the water spots.

In fact, my summer had gone from a five—okay, a zero—to something a whole lot better over the past few weeks. Sure, I'd racked up a criminal charge, but I'd managed to start my own business, complete a handful of jobs, and earn actual money. Ashlyn and I may have had a small, minuscule, infinitesimal misunderstanding, but it seemed we were on the road to reconciliation, which, if I was really lucky, would begin at Sol Jam. Ash and I hadn't exchanged any more emails, but I knew she'd make good on her invitation to see each other. The truest part of me needed to believe that, to believe that she was ready to accept that all I wanted to do was protect her.

Blanche had been a glittering, lovely surprise. I found myself hoping more than once that she'd extend her visit and just stay forever. I may never have a real, maternal relationship with my stepmother, but my stepgrandmother was awesome, and I wasn't going to take her generosity for granted. She made me want to keep going, keep making good choices, even when the deck was stacked against me. She'd also given me some insight into how Belén ticked, which I was starting to see was worth its weight in gold. I wasn't sure exactly how I'd use it, but I'd promised Blanche I'd try. And I would.

"Is there any more dusting spray?" Tilly called from downstairs. I checked the cabinet and found a new can. I wiped the last of the counter clean, picked up the caddy of supplies, and headed downstairs to my next bathroom.

"Here you go," I said, handing the can to Tilly, who was surveying the living room.

"Thanks."

I glided a finger across the glass-smooth coffee table. "I think you missed a spot."

"Is my mother rubbing off on you?" she asked with a laugh.

Making jokes with Tilly, hanging out and giggling together, and going on a sort-of road trip—these were the things I'd always dreamed of doing with a sister, but had never imagined the one who lived with me could be a viable option. Tilly was definitely on my list of good things.

There was still a gaping trench between my father and me—an ocean, in fact—but I'd also promised Blanche that I'd talk with him. He was my dad. He had to love me, no matter what, right? Blanche's belief in me gave me some hope that my dad would let go of his disappointment and start to see for himself that I had simply gotten stuck in a bad situation, not made a bad choice.

Taking a short break from my chores, I grabbed my phone to dash off a quick email.

Hi Dad,

Just wanted to tell you I'm glad you're coming home soon. I can't wait to tell you more about
what I've been up to all summer. It might be a long
conversation—brace yourself. I miss you.

Love,
Tatum

I took a selfie, flashing my dad a smile and pretending
to wave at him, attached it to the email, and pressed *send*.
I hoped he would take notice that I wasn't scowling or
smirking.

Aside from the handful of emails, we hadn't actually
spoken since I'd hung up on him; he'd always managed
to call when I was out. My good mood was forcing my
guilt over our last conversation to show itself. Maybe this
letter—and the ones before, where I had initiated the contact to show him I cared—would soften things a little bit
for his homecoming. A girl could hope.

After I finished the bathrooms and took the vacuum out
of the closet, Blanche emerged from the basement.

"Good morning, ladies," she called. "Who wants
bagels for breakfast? I don't feel like cooking."

"Me," I called. Tilly cheered from the hall, where she
was almost done sweeping.

"Good choice, girls. I'll be back shortly." Blanche
took the spare car keys from the spare key drawer and slid

her leopard-printed purse over her shoulder. "The house smells nice and clean, Tatum." She winked and disappeared into the garage.

I vacuumed as fast as I could, taking care to make the marks in the carpet that Belén left after she was done. The more evidence, the better. Afterward, I sliced open a cinnamon crunch bagel, courtesy of Blanche, smeared it with cream cheese, and took my breakfast up to my room so I could shower and pick out the perfect show-time outfit.

When I came back into my room post-shower, smelling much sweeter and wrapped in a towel, I found the prettiest sundress ever on my bed, and a note lying on top. It was the same paper Tilly's note had been written on.

> All my bunco winnings were burning a hole in my pocket. I thought Cinderella could use a new gown for the ball.
>
> All my love,
> Blanche

I held it to my body and looked in the mirror. The blue-and-white seersucker halter dress had a swingy A-line skirt and pockets, falling just to the tops of my knees. My arms and shoulders were glowing bronze from the hours spent outside and, just like Hunter, my biceps were more defined than they'd ever been in my life. My hair now fell well past my shoulders, highlighted naturally, also thanks to the blazing sun. As I stepped into the dress, I looked down and saw a new pair of silver sandals, more delicate than my old ones, sitting at the foot of my bed. I slipped my feet into them, ran some gloss over my lips, and grabbed my purse.

Blanche was waiting for me at the kitchen table.

"You look lovely, Tatum."

I smiled at my new sandals. "Thank you, Blanche. This was so generous. *You* are so generous."

"It was nothing."

"It was everything." I bent and kissed her cheek.

She blushed and smiled. "I hope you have the time of your life, my dear."

Tilly descended the stairs, and we went over the itinerary with Blanche once again. I even double-checked the mileage on the car and wrote it down for her, though she insisted it wasn't necessary. I insisted it was.

"Please be home by midnight, girls. My only request."

"We will," I promised.

Blanche hugged us both and shooed us out the door and on our way to pampering, camaraderie, and a little musical bliss.

Chapter 16

*H*unter hadn't been kidding when he said the owner of the property for Sol Jam had a lot of space. In Arlington, our houses were practically on top of each other, but out here in the country—which sounded funny, since it was only about forty or so miles away—it was easy to forget the gridlock, the hurried anxiety, and the apathy of a major metropolitan area. The address our GPS directed us toward was down a gravel road, way in the back of a street that had me wondering if a wayward cow might appear any minute.

"Is this the same state we came from?" Tilly wondered out loud.

"I was just thinking the same thing."

The bumping and jostling finally gave way to a huge mansion sitting atop green grass that seemed to go on forever. I had no idea that much space still existed on private property this close to the city. It was, though, the ideal place for a group of rock-star hopefuls to spend a warm summer evening banging on drums and wailing on a guitar without causing law enforcement to show up.

Tilly parked the car in the circular driveway behind Abby's brother's Camaro, and I was almost blinded by the sunlight glinting off its chrome bumper. Satchel over my shoulder, loaded with laptop, camera, and business swag, I headed for the backyard with Tilly trailing behind me, both of us gaping at the oversized wedding cake of a house. We stopped in our tracks when we saw the setup.

I'd been expecting the bands to perform on a patio, with the audience on blankets and maybe a few lawn chairs, but there was an honest-to-goodness stage on the property. Someone handy with a hammer had made a large platform raised several feet off the ground, with scaffolding around the edges, speakers hanging strategically. What looked like a string of twinkle lights had been wrapped around the metal frame, which I bet would look quite festive once the sun went down. Two guys—a little older than me, maybe seniors or college students—were plugging in all sorts of complicated-looking electrical cords and arranging instruments and stands on the stage.

Out in the yard, edged with dense trees, blankets and large pillows all the colors of the rainbow had been strewn about. They looked almost as comfortable as the Schmidts' couch. A wooden gazebo, also draped with lights, sat at the far end of the yard, and a fire pit flanked with benches was off to the side.

"I think I'm just going to park myself here all night,"

I said to Tilly, pointing to an enormous burgundy pillow resting on a navy blanket.

She poked me in the shoulder. "Don't you have work to do?"

I rolled my eyes. "Yeah, yeah, yeah. I guess Abby would be mad if I ditched her to lie around." Like she'd heard her name, Abby emerged from a sliding glass door right behind the stage.

"Hey! You made it!" She gave us a big wave and propped her sunglasses up on her head.

"Hey, Abby. This is my stepsister, Tilly. Tilly, this is Abby, my partner in plant removal."

Abby's dark brown eyebrows shot up. I hadn't prepped her for Tilly; I thought the element of surprise might be more fun. "Right. Tilly. Good to meet you." They shook hands, and Tilly smiled warmly. Abby relaxed. "So, the other bands are trickling in, and there are some guys in the basement warming up. Hunter's in there with them."

"What about Kyle and Paolo? And the one who was on vacation?" I looked around the yard, but no one else appeared.

"Paolo is on his way. Kyle and Shay have some school photo thing, they'll be here later."

"Are they McIntosh students? Senior pictures started today," Tilly said.

"Yeah, do you know them?" Abby ran a hand through her curls.

"No, I don't think so. None of those names sound familiar. I don't really get out of my ballet bubble very often, though. If they're in the music program, we wouldn't have crossed paths often."

"Ballet bubble? You do have a sense of humor!" I bumped Tilly with my shoulder, and she bumped me back.

"I'm trying it on for size."

Abby, Tilly, and I sat down in the middle row of blankets to stake our claim, falling into comfortable small talk. I was thankful for Abby's ability to charm anyone, though Tilly held her own. Other music-lovers of all ages started showing up with picnic baskets and lawn chairs, spreading out in front of the stage to wait for the entertainment to begin.

I kept checking my phone, hoping for a text from Ashlyn, but nothing came. I convinced myself that she was still coming and that perhaps Blue Valley didn't allow cell phones, or maybe her dad had confiscated it when she'd gotten in trouble. When a decent-sized crowd had gathered and multiple members of other bands had made their rounds of the stage, Hunter finally emerged from the house and made a beeline for us.

He plopped down so close to Abby, their hips touched. I saw her instantly melt in his direction, and resisted calling them out. I knew I shouldn't laugh; they were cute in all of their awkward flirtishness.

"Are you nervous?" Abby looked at Hunter like no one else was around.

"Yeah, definitely. Last year we did this on a whim, but now we have legit fans. People are coming specifically to hear us. That's a lot of pressure." He ran his hands through his blond hair several times like he didn't know what else to do with them. His foot jittered under his crossed legs. I hoped Abby would give him a hug soon.

She did the next best thing—distraction. Abby held up her reporter's notebook next to her face and grinned. "So is there anything else I should know about this concert? You know, for the article and all."

I rolled my eyes in Tilly's direction, the ghost of a smile appearing on her lips.

"Owen, who owns the house, is this hilarious, former-hippie type. Except he's loaded, hence the house and property. His son's band, which started Sol Jam, is on after us. I just talked to Owen inside, actually. He's going to come out and give a speech." Hunter shook his head. "He's a wacky dude, for sure."

He adjusted his position to a crouch, knees jutting out like a frog's. "I need to get back, actually. The other guys should be here soon, and we'll need to warm up a little. We're doing something new tonight for the first time."

I saluted him. "Good luck and Godspeed, my friend."

Tilly just smiled.

Abby grabbed Hunter's hand and squeezed. "You'll be fantastic. How could you not?" He winked at her and jogged back into the house.

"That's it? No good luck kiss?" I mock-shoved her.

"Seriously? Do you think I should have? He wouldn't have run away screaming?"

"Abby, I think Hunter would appreciate anything you offer him, be it a kiss or a grand gesture. That boy is smitten."

Her cheeks colored, and she smiled shyly to herself. "Maybe you're right."

I shook my head and just laughed at her. Moments later, as Hunter predicted, a rather round man with a long gray beard stepped onto the stage and started tapping the mic. He wore an obnoxious Hawaiian shirt, long board shorts, white athletic socks, and black Velcro sandals.

"Is this thing on? Testing, testing." Feedback screeched and crackled; I covered my ears until he backed up. The man took the mic out of the stand and smiled. "Great. Hi, everyone. In case you're new here, I'm Owen. I live there." He pointed to the house, and I couldn't help but giggle. He welcomed us to the concert and thanked us for supporting young artists. "We've been doing this thing here for several years now, and I'm so proud of how it's gotten bigger and better each summer. Some people ask me how I justify spending so much on this concert and keeping it free. I like to say I charge a finder's fee when any of these talented groups of kids signs a recording con-tract." He chuckled, and the audience erupted in laughter.

"You think I'm kidding. With the groups we have here tonight, I just might not be far off from that goal." He winked, and encouraged us to roast the marshmallows and hot dogs he'd provided over by the fire pit.

"We're totally doing that," I said, rubbing my tummy. Owen waved at the crowd one more time and ushered five terrified-looking kids on stage.

The first three bands were decent, but nothing special or memorable. There were a million bands and singers just like them on the radio, pumping out millions-earning singles and then fading away. I was glad my friends had an original sound.

I turned backward and scanned the crowd, hoping to catch a glimpse of Ashlyn's face, but all I saw was a sea of strangers—happy strangers, but no Ash. My good mood diminished a little bit.

"Are you ready?" Abby grabbed my arm and shook when it was time for the Frisson to play.

"Ab, calm yourself. It's not the sixties, and they're not the Beatles."

"Oh, I've always been more of a Stones girl."

I laughed. "Maybe Hunter will do some Jagger swagger."

As if I'd called to him, Hunter took the stage. Any signs of nerves from earlier had fled, and in place of the anxious boy was a confident young man, ready to command the microphone. He'd slicked his floppy hair into a faux hawk and changed into a plain black T-shirt and jeans. He was barefoot, which I thought was a bold move on the wooden stage, but if he wasn't afraid of splinters, more power to him. To his right, Kyle stood, surly as always, hand on his bass, scowling at the crowd.

Tilly leaned over and whispered in my ear, "I recognize the bass player. I think he used to go out with one of the dancers in my program."

"Really? He seems like he doesn't really like people," I whispered back, and then smiled to myself. Whispering with Tilly was nice.

Paolo and his drum kit were elevated on a smaller platform at the back of the stage. He was the antithesis of Kyle, a big goofy grin on his face, wavy golden-brown hair sweeping his brows. I turned my eyes to the elusive fourth member, seated at the upright piano someone had wheeled out on stage, and sucked in a sharp breath. This time, I grabbed Abby's arm.

"Ab, that's Shay?"

She looked at me like I'd lost my marbles. "Yes," she said slowly. "Why? You look like you've seen a ghost."

"I kind of did. Do you remember that conversation we had about missed opportunities way back at the beginning of summer?"

"Sure."

"That's him. Shay is the guy from the showcase."

"No way! He's your hot guy? Small world."

I didn't know whether to sit up straighter and hope he noticed me, shrink back and hide under a pillow, or jump up and down and wave my arms, yelling "Hey, remember me?" I did none of the above, but sat there frozen in place, waiting for the music to start.

"Hey, everyone, how are you feeling tonight? We are, proudly, the Frisson." Hunter's stance at the microphone was natural, like he was born to be on stage. I looked over at Abby, her eyes focused on him and his on her. The crowd, a veritable ocean of people, clapped and whooped. They clearly had some fans. "Thank you so much for coming. We appreciate the support and love seeing so many familiar faces. We're going to start with one of our favorites."

Paolo clacked his drum sticks together loudly and Shay started tapping out the opening notes of what I quickly recognized as *Where's Summer B?* by Ben Folds Five. A quirky classic and the perfect opening number, it got all four guys singing and oo-oo-ooing into their mics. The crowd immediately responded by singing along with them, and before I knew it, the laid-back concert had turned into an enthusiastic party. Hunter took the microphone out of its stand and marched back and forth as the guys behind him swayed and tapped their toes while singing. Paolo and Kyle were into it, but Shay was mesmerizing. He was so happy, dancing at his piano and making overexaggerated faces while he played; the stage was his element, and during the complicated piano solo, the audience responded with clapping and hollering. In some ways, his bouncy, joyful performance was more captivating than Hunter's strutting. I couldn't look anywhere else but at him.

When the song ended, I clapped wildly, cheering as loudly as I could. I felt a smattering of privilege that I knew these guys, and was proud to be taking part in working to get them some more recognition. I hoped the article Abby would write would be successful. How could it not be?

"I'm going to go up closer to take some pictures. Tatum, take notes." Abby hopped up and dusted off her shorts.

"Me too, if you don't mind. Their drummer's cute." Tilly stood up, while Abby and I exchanged a look asking *Who is this girl?* Abby shrugged.

"Sure, you can help." They strolled off together toward the stage, leaving me to lounge on the pillows with my notebook and pen.

As the next song began, something folksy I didn't recognize, I felt a light tap on my shoulder that jolted me back to the blanket and out of the world happening on stage. I snapped my head around, mostly out of surprise but a little bit from annoyance that my happy escape was being interrupted, and saw Ashlyn kneeling behind me.

She was a slightly faded version of herself. A little less blonde, no makeup, and her blue eyes, sans the mischievous sparkle I was used to, didn't quite meet mine. When she withdrew her arm, I noticed her hand was shaking. "Hey." Ash was many things, but timid wasn't one of them. Was she afraid to talk to me?

"Hey, Ash. I wasn't sure you were still coming." I resisted checking my watch for the time.

"Yeah, we had some car trouble. I wanted to be here for the opener, but it didn't happen." She didn't look at me when she spoke, like she was nervous about what I might say or do. The friendly tone of our last email exchange seemed a thing of the past now that we were finally face to face after two months apart.

Knowing she wouldn't have said she missed me if she hadn't meant it, I held out an olive branch. "Well, better late than never." I thought about hugging her, but it seemed too soon, and judging by how she was acting, I was scared she might stiffen from my touch.

Thankfully, Ash brightened, but she kept her lashes trained to the blanket. At another deafening uproar from the crowd, I glanced back at the stage, where the boys were playing the last lingering strains of their song. None of the earlier bands had gotten so much praise. My heart swelled a little for them.

"So how's school? Were you taking summer classes?" I figured this was a safe topic. Maybe she'd let her cocoon of what looked like embarrassment open a little.

Ash lifted her head and finally looked at me. "Yeah, but nothing too serious. An SAT prep class and an art history elective. We took a lot of trips into DC to the galleries." It didn't escape me that she'd have to drive right by Arlington on her way into the city. Did she think about me as she passed?

"I'm sure your dad must be thrilled you've had a productive summer." I didn't try to hide my sarcasm, hoping it would make Ashlyn laugh.

Her head went back down. "Yeah, he's not really thrilled about much these days."

I smiled wryly. "Neither are my parents. I feel your pain."

"What do they have to be upset about?"

"Oh, you know, my criminal record. My cavorting with miscreants. The storm cloud of disappointment that lives over our house because of me. Basically, my typical Wednesday. It's better than it was at the beginning of the summer, though, and my dad will be home soon. I'm trying to be the bigger person, actually. Not be such a brat."

Ash's cheeks flamed, and I wondered if I shouldn't have been so brutally honest. She started picking at her cuticles, a sure sign of distress. She took a long, deep breath and fisted her hands in her lap. "But you didn't do anything wrong."

All the air left my lungs. For what felt like an eternity, I'd wanted her to say that. Wanted her to *believe* it. I knew it was true, but hearing it from her lips felt like vindication. At least partly. I took a breath, as long as she had. "I'm glad you said that. I needed to hear it."

She smiled sadly. "I'm sorry it took me so long."

"Better late than never," I said for the second time that night.

"So it's been awful?" Her voice was tiny, full of regret.

"Yep. Pretty much. I've spent most of the summer afraid you hated me. My dad left the country for an assignment after telling me I've disappointed him. Belén put me on her version of house arrest. I'm only here tonight because of Blanche and Tilly." I smiled. "Tilly and I are becoming friendly, if you can believe that. She's up there." I pointed to her crouched down by the stage.

Tears pooled in the corner of Ash's eyes. "I'm so, so sorry, Tate. I didn't know. I promise I didn't know. I was so embarrassed, and I just reacted. It was easier for me to direct that anger at you than myself, unfortunately, and you didn't deserve it. I'm sorry I was so awful to you. I've really missed you," she whispered as the tears came streaming down. This time, without thinking, I scooted over and put my arm around her and held her tightly. She put her forehead down on my shoulder and sobbed quietly as the Frisson played the pop cover I'd heard at band practice. It felt odd to be comforting a crying Ash during such an upbeat song.

"It's okay. I forgive you. I missed you too. I know you didn't know what he was going to do." She sniffled into my shoulder. "I know this has been a bad summer—for you too, obviously."

She lifted her head. "You have no idea. My parents have all but disowned me. And the girls at school are so mean and snobby. I don't know how I'm going to survive a full school year."

"Maybe you can make your case again to your dad?" When I thought about Mr. Zanotti's choice to send Ash away, I knew I'd been the lucky one between the two of us. But I also knew that if I could be swayed to change my mind about Belén, he could certainly forgive his daughter.

She shrugged sadly. "Maybe."

"Either way, let's make a deal. Next time you feel a magnetic pull toward a guy that gives me the creeps, you'll listen when I tell you he's bad news. Okay?"

She smiled. "I think I can do that."

"And if we get into another fight or disagreement, about anything at all, we don't let months go by before we talk it out. And also, let's not get the courts involved."

"Deal." We both laughed, and she hugged me back.

"It's going to get better. Look at us—it already has." I could only hope Mr. Zanotti would come around, or that Ash would figure out some way to get through to him. Like I hoped to with my dad and Belén.

Ashlyn laid her head back on my shoulder and I rested my head on top of hers. We sat that way, still and connected, through the next song.

"They're really good."

"Definitely. Actually, I know them. I went to one of their practices—" I stopped talking when Shay sauntered up to Hunter's microphone and tapped it with his finger.

"Hey, everyone." His smile was easy, and I immediately smiled back in his direction. Talk about magnetic pull.

"Thanks again for coming. Even though we'd all still play music for ourselves because we love it so much, it makes it even better when there's someone listening who

loves it too." A lot of kids sitting in the crowd nodded.
"So on that note, pun totally intended"—he laughed at
his own joke—"the guys have graciously agreed to let me
do something a little self-indulgent tonight. For our last
song, I put together something special for someone who is
here tonight and who also loves music. So much that she
once said my playing wrecked her."

I didn't think twice about what he said until he
walked to the side of the stage and brought over a cello,
while Hunter brought him a chair to sit on. My mouth
popped open, and all the blood rushed to my ears. As he
started to play, the melody I'd listened to so many times,
the one that I'd memorized through sound and through
tears, came soaring out of his instrument.

I blinked several times in disbelief. SK was Shay was
my hot guy? How was that possible?

I stared at him, at the bow moving so beautifully across
the strings, as the emotion I'd felt so strongly in my chest
played out on his handsome face. He'd closed his eyes, but
his brows and lips—which I couldn't help but notice looked
like they might be soft—were expressing the same longing
I'd felt when I heard his recording. I closed my eyes too
and just listened. On its own, my hand found Ashlyn's and
gripped it tightly as the notes swelled.

"Do you know this song?" she whispered, concerned.

"Yes," I whispered back. I opened my eyes in time
to see SK open his, which were focused right on me. He
knew it was me; he knew who I was. How had this happened? And without me realizing? I felt like I'd just been
transported to some alternate universe where everything I

thought I knew was wrong. Maybe that wouldn't be such a bad thing. I stared right back at him, unable to process the thoughts swirling around my head. I was grateful for Ashlyn's hand, which must have been aching from my viselike grip.

As SK continued to play, the other band members took their places back at their instruments and joined him, mashing the classical solo piece with a Sarah Jarosz bluegrass song I'd come to love this summer thanks to SK, "Tell Me True."

Even though it was Hunter singing, I felt in my veins it was SK asking if I thought of him, if there was a chance. Though we'd been thousands of miles apart, both in distance and situation, over the course of the summer, I couldn't deny now that all the times I'd thought he'd been flirting with me were real. I hadn't fooled myself into thinking his words had double meanings. My stomach knotted in the best possible way, knowing that the tiny-something-nameless feeling I'd felt had also been felt by the person on the other end. I hadn't allowed myself to think about that possibility, it seemed so unreal, but in that moment, there was nothing else on my mind.

"This might be the best song I've ever heard." Ash squeezed my hand, somehow knowing the music was affecting me more than it was her.

"Me too."

When the song ended, all four boys stood in a line on stage and took a bow as the entire audience jumped to their feet and clapped like their lives depended on it. I did the same, pulling Ash up with me. Even though the night was warm, I shivered on my feet, musing over what, if anything, to do next. The boys exited the stage as the last and final band began tuning their instruments. Abby and Tilly finally came back, both with enormous smiles on their faces, chattering together about the music.

"So good!" Abby said. Tilly nodded her head vigorously in agreement. They both seemed to notice Ashlyn at the same time.

"Hi, Tilly," Ash said quietly, hand in the air in greeting.

"Hello, Ashlyn." Tilly pursed her lips primly. I didn't know if it was out of disapproval for Ash or protection of me. I hoped the latter. I nodded slightly so Tilly would know everything was cool with me and Ash, and she visibly relaxed her jaw.

"Ashlyn, you know Abby Gold from school, right?"

She nodded. "Yeah, I think we had math together freshman year."

Abby gave her best professional smile. "I think that's right. Thanks for coming. I know the support is appreciated. Did you all get a chance to catch up?" She looked at me pointedly.

"Yeah, we did." I smiled and glanced at Ash, who seemed happier than she had all night.

Abby's face suddenly broke out into a wide grin as she focused on something behind me. "Hey, Shay! Amazing show. You guys really outdid yourselves."

I froze as SK came up behind us and gave Abby a quick side hug. "Thanks, Abby. And thanks for coming, ladies. We definitely have the prettiest fans." He smiled at me, and I was glad for the darkness concealing my furious blush. "Could I borrow you for a minute, Tate?"

He called me Tate. Abby's eyebrows perked up. "Sure," I said, and gingerly took the hand he extended toward me, like it was something we'd been doing forever. As he led me away from my friends, I sent a quick "oh my goodness" look over my shoulder at them and tried not to swoon too hard at the thought of his hand—warm, firm, calloused—holding mine.

"Is this okay?" I blinked at the sound of his voice. He held up our entwined fingers.

"Oh. Um, yes." Majorly surreal that I was hand in hand with someone who, until an hour ago, had been a figment of my imagination, but definitely okay.

He laughed softly. "I thought we could roast some marshmallows. You do like roasted marshmallows, don't you?"

"Of course I do. Who doesn't?"

"Well, that's a relief. Because I don't think I could handle a girl who didn't like them."

I sucked in a breath. Flirting in person was so much better than over the internet. His teasing nearly knocked me off my feet. My fingers twitched, and he held them tighter.

We arrived at the fire pit, flames dancing in the light breeze, and he let go of my hand so he could retrieve two sticks and a bag of jumbo marshmallows. The instant he broke contact, I wished he hadn't.

SK stuck a marshmallow on a stick and handed it to me. "Here you go."

"Thank you." I was still so surprised he was here in the flesh, I didn't know what else to say.

He made one for himself and sat down next to me on a bench before we stuck our marshmallows into the fire.

"So, are you a lightly toasted fan, or do you like it charred and dripping?" he asked. I could hear the smile in his voice. "Because I myself like my marshmallows somewhere in the middle. Gooey so the sugar starts to caramelize, but not all blackened and falling off the stick."

"You sound like an expert."

"Well, I have been on a camping trip or two."

"Cub scouts?" I teased.

"You know, I look really good in khaki."

"I bet." He probably looked good in everything.

We sat in comfortable silence for a while, watching the fire lick the air. I pulled my marshmallow out first.

"Brown," I said, smiling shyly at him.

"Brown." He nodded knowingly.

Mine was perfectly crisp; I licked my lips. He licked his as well, and we both stuffed our faces with the sugary deliciousness. When I'd finished chewing, I felt ready to burst. There was so much I needed to know.

"So, how did you know it was me? I mean, I was me? When did you know?" I blurted.

"Honestly, I didn't figure it out until rehearsal last week. Abby was there, and said something about how Tatum the graphic designer, who made the poster, was sneaking out to the show."

I smacked my hand on the bench. "Of course, me sneaking out would tip you off."

"Well, that's how I knew the girl I'd been emailing all summer was going to see us play. I didn't realize we'd met in person before until right before we went on stage. Hunter pointed you out, and it all clicked. Like a ton of bricks, as they say."

"I hope you didn't get hurt."

"Nah, I'm pretty solid." He knocked on his head as I remembered smacking into him at McIntosh and exactly how solid he was.

"I feel like so silly for not connecting the dots earlier."

"How could you have? I never told you my name when we bumped into each other at the art showcase."

I flushed yet again, recalling how we'd originally met. "You could have told me it was your poster I was shredding, you know?"

He laughed. "But you were so cute when you were giving your honest opinions. I couldn't break your heart and tell you how close you were to the performer himself." He ran a finger over the top of my hand; I may have shuddered a little.

"So, performer. Who are you in real life? SK? Shay? What do you want me to call you?" I hid behind my lashes.

"Perhaps now would be a good time to reintroduce myself." He stuck his hand out confidently. "Seamus Kipsang. Pleased to meet you."

"Tatum Elsea. Charmed." I gave him my hand, and he squeezed it. "Gosh, if I'd asked for a little more information, I might have realized you were you way earlier. The night I snuck out to band practice, maybe."

"Or if I'd had the guts to ask you for your number in the first place."

"That too." We both laughed, and he threaded his

fingers through mine again. For the first time since we'd sat down, I noticed the band on stage. They were good, but definitely not as good as the Frisson. We listened together, hand in hand, just enjoying the moment.

When the song ended, Seamus turned to me. "What did you think of your song?"

My song. "Wrecked again. I'm surprised you didn't find a puddle of me on the ground afterward."

He grinned. "That's good, right?"

"Yes, very good. I loved it. How did you have time to do that, anyway? I mean, if you only knew this week that I'd be here?"

"Truth? I started on the arrangement while I was in Ireland. I dunno, I felt inspired, I guess." This time, he blushed. It was adorable. "I like to think I would have had the courage to send it to you, and then you would have demanded we meet in person. But this worked out even better, I think."

"Demanded, eh?"

"You did ask me a lot of rather bossy questions."

"True." I watched as the firelight reflected golden flickers in his green eyes. "I have to ask you something I've been wondering ever since I first heard you perform."

"What's that?"

"You don't have to tell me if it's too personal, but I am dying to know what you think about when you play. The look on your face is unbelievable. I could feel it in the recording too. So many emotions."

He suddenly became shy. "It's not too personal," he said, but I knew it was something important by his small voice. "I actually think about my parents." Not the answer I was expecting. "You know how I told you my mom's from Ireland and my dad's from Kenya?" I nodded. "So my dad told me how they met at a dance club, of all places. He was studying at GW and my mom was at NYU. She was down in DC for the weekend, visiting a friend, and, to make a long story short, he pretty much saved her from some skeevy guy who wanted to dance with her and wouldn't leave her alone. He pretended to be her boyfriend, and that was that."

I laughed. "That's awesome. But how does that translate to your playing?"

"They dated long-distance until they graduated, and my dad went back to Kenya to take care of visas and stuff, and it was really hard for both of them to be apart. They knew, right away, they wanted to be together, but because of life, they couldn't."

"Oh."

"Yeah. So that's what I think about when I'm playing the wistful, bittersweet pieces." He offered me a small smile. "I think I might get it now."

I smiled back, fully prepared to faint dead away onto the ground.

The band finished up and the crowd began to disperse, and still we sat, hand in hand. When I saw Tilly inching her way toward us, clearly trying to not interrupt the moment we were having, I checked my watch. "I'm probably going to turn into a pumpkin soon. We promised we would be home by midnight."

Seamus stood up and pulled me up off the bench,

dangerously close to an embrace. "Well, princess, then I guess this is good night." I didn't want it to be. I so didn't. It must have shown on my face, because the corners of his mouth lifted jovially. "But before you go, I have a question."

"Yes?" I breathed.

"Could I interest you in a real date some time?"

My smile could not have gotten any wider.

"Definitely. I demand it. Though, that will probably involve meeting my parents." I stiffened at the thought of bringing Seamus home and introducing him to the family. Would I even be allowed out of the house? I wondered what my dad and Belén would think.

"Don't worry, I'm great with parents." He flashed me a million-watt smile like he was appearing in a toothpaste commercial, waggling his eyebrows.

"It's not you I'm worried about," I said, but I laughed anyway. He wrapped me up in his arms for a hug, and I marveled at how well our bodies fit together. He was warm against me, and I could feel his heart beating, just as fast as mine was, against my chest. I pulled away first and smiled, a real, genuine, eye-crinkling smile. He gave me one back and brought my hand, again entwined with his, to his lips. I closed my eyes, and when he let me go, I could still feel the sparks on the back of my hand.

"I wish I'd done that back in June," he said, with a smile that glowed in the darkness.

"Me too," I murmured, and caught myself. "I mean, uh, I wanted, I mean . . . ." I threw my hands up. "I can never speak around you. I turn into incoherent girl."

He chuckled and put his arm around my shoulder. "I know, I kinda like it." We disconnected, and he patted his hips. "I almost forgot. I think this is yours." He unclipped something from his belt loop, took my hand, and pressed a small, warm object into my palm. When I looked down, there was my missing keychain.

I froze. Just when I thought the night couldn't have gotten any stranger, my most sentimental possession, the one I thought had vanished forever, showed back up in exactly the most unexpected place.

I studied it, winking in the reflection of the fairy lights in the yard. After a summer of self-reflection, I knew I didn't need a piece of metal to keep me out of harm's way. I could do that all by myself. But it was still a reminder—a good reminder—of my mother, of my father, and of the fact that I wasn't on my own. I'd thought I had no one on my side when I'd lost the keychain, but now I had Abby and Hunter. I had Ash back, and Tilly for the first time. And somehow, as if by fate, it seemed I had Seamus. I didn't need the keychain now, other than to simply hold my keys, but I was glad to have it back just the same. I glanced at it again, ran a thumb over the inscription, and slipped it into my pocket. I looked up at Seamus and cocked my head to the side.

"Where did you find this?"

"At school. The night we met. It was on the floor, right under my poster."

"The angel wings on my TLC logo didn't give me away?"

He smiled at me warmly. "I hoped it was you." He pulled me in again and pressed a light kiss into my hair. "Good night, Tatum."

"Good night, Seamus."

I walked, slightly dazed, back to my friends. Tilly had packed up my belongings for me and was standing amiably with Ashlyn. Abby watched the stage, where Hunter was helping break down the electricals, and scribbled in her notebook. She turned at my footsteps.

"Hello, friend, welcome back," Abby said, giving me a knowing look.

I opened my mouth to dish, but Ash interrupted me. "Tate, I want to hear all about whatever that was." She waved her hands in the general direction of the fire pit. "Because it looked like something swoonworthy just happened. But my ride is about to leave. I'll be home Labor Day weekend. Can we talk then? Hang out?" Hope hung in her words.

"Absolutely. I won't leave out anything." I grabbed Ash and pressed on her the fiercest hug I could manage, hoping I communicated all the things I was feeling—relief, optimism, affection for her—into our embrace. She hugged me back; we clung together until tears snuck down both our cheeks and mingled together.

We pulled apart and giggled at each other. "I'll see you soon, Ash."

"Soon."

Ashlyn squeezed my hand and ran across the yard, toward the cars and into the darkness. My heart swelled with happiness.

*O*n the ride home from Sol Jam, I made Tilly promise she would show her mom the new portfolio. If I was going to explain myself once more and go down in flames, she was going with me.

"You can't wait," I told her. "She's going to need some time to accept it."

Tilly gave me a grim smile. "Yeah, she's never really been good with change."

"Again with the humor! I am a good influence on you, stepsister."

We drove home the rest of the way, going over every detail of what had happened that night, from the band to Ashlyn to Seamus to Tilly's sudden interest in Paolo. It felt like we'd been having these kinds of conversations for years.

After we crept into the dark house and tiptoed upstairs, I slid into my pajamas, replaying the unbelievable series of events that had transpired with a smile on my face so bright, people could see it next door. I was almost asleep when my laptop dinged. One more happy surprise—there in my inbox was a note from Seamus. I brought the computer over to my bed, laid down, and set it on my stomach to read.

> Hi Tate,
>
> So, I just left you an hour ago, and I'm writing this from the car on the drive home.

My heart started thumping.

> I had the best time and couldn't wait to tell you. I hope that isn't creepy of me. I promise I'm not a stalker. Just ignore the devilishly handsome guy lurking outside your window.

I giggled. The last thing I would do if he was outside was ignore him.

> In all seriousness, I couldn't have asked for a better night. When can we do it again?
>
> Yours in music and
> marshmallows,
> Seamus

I let out a loud yelp and slapped my hands over my mouth. It was the best valediction yet.

> P.S.—A friend just sent me this video and some photos from tonight. Take a look. Something to use for the site?

I wrote him back right away.

Immediately, if not sooner. Please.

I opened the attachments and found several gorgeous shots of Seamus, seated with his cello between his legs, playing my song. The simultaneous pain and joy written on his face in the picture hit me just as hard as it had in person, and I found myself compelled to listen to him playing "Chaconne" on repeat. No longer something to make me cry; the grin never left my face until I fell asleep.

The next morning, I gleefully filled Blanche in on the highlights of the evening, Tilly at my side.

"I don't know how to repay you. Honestly." I hugged her just as tightly as I had hugged Ashlyn the night before.

"The smile on your face is enough thanks, Tatum. And you had a good time?" Blanche shifted her gazed between Tilly and me.

"We had an amazing time, Abuela. The music was beautiful. The company was good." Tilly's brown eyes sparkled mischievously. "I think Tatum especially liked the view of the piano and cello."

I dropped my jaw, and she laughed. I smacked her playfully in the arm. "I don't remember you complaining about the view of the drum kit."

Tilly gave me a tight-lipped, secretive smile.

Blanche shook her head, amused. "I'm glad it was worth it, Tatum. You deserved it. You too, Matilda. It's nice to see you girls happy. I think the night off was just what you both needed."

I hugged her again. "Can you please stay forever?"

She laughed, a silvery tinkle. "I don't know if my daughter would agree to that. But, I think I could manage more frequent visits."

"Yes please."

"And now that I've upheld my end of the bargain, you must complete yours."

I held my breath. My dad would be home soon, and there was no way of getting out of facing my fears. "I know. Think some positive thoughts for me?"

She patted my head. "You'll be fine."

Tilly cleared her throat. "Don't forget, you're not the only one who has things to share, Tatum."

I looked over, and our eyes locked. I was glad to not have to jump into the deep end of the pool alone.

Two days later, and my dad's plane was scheduled to touch down in the late afternoon. I hadn't slept much the night before, planning out all the things I wanted to say and reviewing them over and over in my head. I hoped I had the courage to calmly and rationally explain how I'd felt when he'd left, and how I was happy with who I was and the decisions I'd made. I wanted to tell him I was proud of how I'd handled the Ashlyn/Chase situation, even if he wasn't, and I was also proud of how I'd changed this summer. I wanted to tick off the items on my list of things I'd come to appreciate, most importantly about our family, over the last few months. I hoped that my effort to be less of a pain to Belén would be a point in my favor. And I definitely needed to apologize for worrying him, for being rude, and for not staying in contact better while he was gone. When we loaded up the car and drove to Dulles Airport, my entire body was buzzing with anxiety, and it was all I could do not to throw up.

As we parked and got out of the car, I lagged back, waiting for Tilly and Blanche to start walking while Belén fussed with her purse. I told myself that this was my last chance to make things right, or as close to right as they were going to get, before my dad was home. When she finally locked the car, I grabbed her elbow in a move that was either smart or laughable.

"Belén?"

She eyed me with surprise. I couldn't remember the last time we touched. "Yes, Tatum?"

I gulped and tried to summon every ounce of bravery and humility I had in me. "I just wanted to say that I'm really sorry for being difficult, um, recently. Actually, always. I know you've just been looking out for me, and I wasn't very nice about it." As I trailed off, her face became unreadable. I held my breath and waited. No matter what she said back to me, even if she ignored my words and walked past me into the terminal, I'd said my piece. The ball was back in her court.

Belén stared at me and stood so still, the only motion was her lungs expanding. And then finally, "Thank you, Tatum. I appreciate you saying that."

Her tone was cool, making my heart fall to the ground. However, just as I'd noticed when she chastised me for sneaking out to band practice, something else lingered underneath Belén's polite words. I didn't expect her to apologize and offer me a warm, motherly hug, but I sensed there was more she wouldn't—or maybe couldn't—say.

"Sure," I mumbled.

Just as I turned to go, Belén reached for my hand, squeezed lightly, then let go and walked confidently toward the airport entrance. My heart bounced back up, and I smiled to myself as I followed.

We resumed a slightly more-comfortable-than-usual silence as we hurried to catch up with Blanche and Tilly, who were studying the arrivals board inside.

To my shock, Belén initiated small talk. "I put a lasagna in the oven for dinner before we left. Do you think your father will be happy with that as his first meal back at home?"

She wanted my opinion? I looked around me to see if pigs with wings were circling my head. Confirming they were not, I said, "Yes, it sounds perfect."

"Good," Belén replied. And with that, we rejoined the rest of our family.

When my dad finally pushed through the double doors from immigration, my knees buckled, and I had to grip the metal railing separating family members from arriving passengers to keep from falling down. Blanche, with her never-failing intuition, placed a hand on the small of my back and steadied me. Dad looked just the same, tall and dependable, the man who worked to better the lives of people all around the world. I hoped he'd be able to extend that mission to me.

When he rounded the barrier, Dad wrapped me in his arms, crushing me to his chest. I couldn't breathe, he was holding me so tight, but I didn't care. It seemed like a good sign.

"Tatum, honey, I owe you an apology." I thought I'd misheard him because my ears were mashed against his shirt. He was basically ignoring everyone else *and* apologizing? "Ashlyn called me yesterday. Said she absolutely had to explain everything before I came home."

Oh. She had? Mr. Zanotti probably wouldn't be happy to see a cell phone bill with a call to Africa on it. I mentally high-fived Ash for taking the risk for me.

I pulled away and looked into his eyes, the same warm brown as mine. "What did she say?" My voice trembled. It must have been pretty enlightening. And convincing.

He pulled me in again and kissed the top of my head, like he had when I was little. I closed my eyes and breathed in his dad-scent: laundry detergent and the peppermint gum he always chewed on planes. "Nothing I didn't already know. This trip gave me a lot of time to think about you, Tatum, and what happened, and I found a lot of clarity about the whole situation. I even had a planned speech for today, ready to go, and then Ashlyn called and it just cemented what I needed to say to you. She told me the truth. She told me how you were the best friend she'd ever had and were always taking care of her, even when she made questionable decisions. Which you'd already told me, and I was too stubborn to give enough weight to at the time."

I couldn't believe this was happening. These were the words I had wished for all summer.

My dad pulled away and looked into my teary face, then pressed me to him once more, murmuring into the top of my head. "I'm sorry, Tatum. I should have fought harder for you. I should have trusted that I raised you to do the right thing and trusted that you did it. That you still do it." I exhaled into the fabric of his shirt. "Can you forgive your dad?"

I nodded into his chest, my hair going all astray from the friction. Tears pricked my eyes. I knew he and I had a lot more we needed to talk about, but in that moment, those words were the only thing I wanted.

We disconnected and smiled at each other. Only then did my dad notice the rest of our family, standing around expectantly. He kissed Belén chastely and hugged Tilly and Blanche.

As we headed toward baggage claim, my dad took my hand and linked it in the crook of his elbow, something he hadn't done in probably a decade. "So what's this I hear about you designing websites?"

I choked out a laugh. "I'll tell you all about it at dinner." And I knew I would. That, and a lot more.

While Tilly and I set the table, we whispered the game plan to each other. I knew it was now or never when it came to confessing the truth. The whole truth about the entire summer. If I was really going to start over with my dad and Belén, I had to stick to my promise to Blanche. Though the idea of coming clean and putting myself in my parents' shoes took all the air out of my lungs when Blanche and I first discussed it, the small steps forward I'd made since then lessened my fear.

"Do you want to go first?" I asked Tilly as she folded the cloth napkins into triangles. "You have less to say."

"Do you want me to go first? What will be less scary for you?"

I could have wept at how normal this felt. My stepsister, no longer cased in ice as I had imagined for years, was putting my needs over her own. I passed her a handful of forks and reached for the water glasses. Would it be better to go first and get it over with? "You know, no. I'll go first. Rip off the Band-Aid." I chuckled to myself as I set a glass at my dad's place. "Maybe you piping up after me will soften the blow."

Once the five of us were sitting around the table, a steaming square of carbtastic, cheesy deliciousness on the plates before us, I cleared my throat. Four sets of eyes swung toward me as if I'd beat on a glass with a knife at a wedding. Too bad Seamus wasn't here for me to kiss; that would've been much nicer.

"So, now that Dad's home, I want to talk about this summer. And my, um, arrest." That word, even after I'd come to terms with my innocence, felt stale and wrong in my mouth. Moving right along. I focused on my father, who was seated at the head of the table, and wished for courage to make it through.

"Dad, I need to thank you for what you said at the airport. You knowing that I was just trying to protect my friend is everything. Everything." He nodded, his eyes crinkling in the corners. "And I also need to tell you that I get it. I get why you were mad. Why you thought I put myself at risk. Why I should have asked for your help. I didn't take the potential consequences from being around someone like Chase seriously, until they weren't potential anymore. That's my fault, and I'm sorry."

I held my breath.

"I forgive you, Tatum," my dad said, without even a nanosecond's hesitation.

I let out my breath, probably too loudly, and Blanche winked at me. My eyes shifted to the other end of the table, where Belén sat. "And I'm sorry for worrying you too, Belén. I won't do it again."

I thought I detected her lower lip quiver, but I wasn't certain. She blinked and said, "I forgive you as well, Tatum."

Blanche's foot nudged mine under the table, probably to point out how she'd been right and I hadn't had any reason to be nervous. I nudged her back and inhaled. I hadn't gotten through the worst part yet.

"I'm glad. That means a lot to me." I met Belén's eyes, focused right on me, and then went back to looking at my lasagna. "Because I have more I need to say. Um, confess actually, Belén."

I couldn't look at her as I recounted the bulleted point list in my head of the times I'd snuck out, including tricking Belén into giving me permission to go to Sol Jam with Tilly. I spilled about my graphic design work, about pet sitting, about writing the article with Abby, and about my plans for the money I had earned. I even threw in a bit about applying to college. I made sure that she understood

I was motivated not only by my need for fun, but also my desire to be more involved at school and with my future.

"I know those things don't make up for the fact that I deceived you, but I thought they were important to mention. I hope you can find it in your heart to forgive me."

Belén was quiet throughout my speech, and remained silent for a good five minutes once I'd finished. I was starting to get worried that I'd caused her to have a coronary, so I finally looked up, and discovered she was watching me. My knees quaked in my seat, bracing for a verbal blow, but it never came.

"Tatum, did you feel you needed to lie to me because you didn't think I would approve?"

I nodded. "Yes."

"I see." Her lip was definitely trembling. "I'm sorry if that was the impression I gave you. My intention has always been, from the day your father and I got married, to protect you."

"I know—"

Belén put a hand up to stop me. "I am aware you think my ideas are harsh."

I would have used a different word than harsh, but I felt grateful she recognized this about herself.

"And if you felt I was being unfair to you, I hope you can understand that I acted in the way that I felt was right. I thought you needed boundaries." Blanche's commentary about parents disagreeing sometimes about what "right" is echoed in my ears.

"I know," I said. "I didn't know it until recently, but I do now. That's why I wanted to say all of this. Needed to say it, really."

Whatever Belén, or my dad, or Tilly, or even Blanche said after this, I felt good that I had gotten it out. Emptied my closet of all the skeletons I had collected over the last two-and-a-half months. I would probably sleep better than I had all summer.

Belén's face had grown pale and blotchy. Her lips were now pursed into a barely there line, clamped so tight it looked painful. Was she having trouble talking? I grew increasingly uncomfortable for her; it got to the point where I was compelled to speak. Help her out, maybe.

"So, I guess, whatever punishment you think is appropriate, I will take, and I won't complain. I promise." I just wanted my dad and Belén to trust me again.

"That's very mature of you, sweetheart," my dad said quietly. He and Belén exchanged a lengthy conversation with their eyes the way only married couples can, and then he nodded at her.

"So, what will it be? Scrubbing the floor with a toothbrush? Rinsing my mouth out with soap?" I couldn't think of much else my stepmother hadn't tried. She'd have to find a new parenting blog to follow, one with more creative consequences.

Belén's face went from white to bright red, but she sat up straight, a commanding presence even when flustered. "I think you and I are even, Tatum."

My jaw dropped. "Really?"

"Really." The smallest trace of a smile graced her lips. "Though I can't say I'm pleased to hear about your duplicitous actions while your father was away, it would be a mistake if I didn't recognize my hand in them."

Again, really? I looked at my dad to confirm I'd heard her right, and caught him trying to cover up a smile. Well, then.

"Thank you," I said, stunned. Blanche nudged me harder under the table, as if to tell me she knew this would happen all along.

"You're welcome. I think this is a good opportunity to start fresh, don't you?" Belén eyed me.

"Yes. Yes," I repeated. I had no idea what a fresh start with my stepmother might look like, but I was willing to take the risk if she was.

Before we could break out the hot cocoa and sing kumbaya, my dad suggested we eat the delicious-looking lasagna before it turned ice cold. Everyone laughed then and dug in. Maybe it was the food and maybe it was what had come before it, but nothing I'd eaten in a long, long time had been so satisfying.

Tilly chose to drop her own bomb while we were eating the cannoli Blanche had picked up at a nearby bakery, recommended by her new bunco besties. Belén took the news about Tilly changing her dance focus surprisingly well. And by well, I mean she didn't throw anything or curse.

"I want to see this online portfolio Tatum has made for you, Matilda," Belén demanded. There was something comforting in her reliable response, despite me being nervous about what her reaction might be. Not only for Tilly, but for myself. Belén hadn't seen any of my art in years.

All five of us clicked through the site, then watched the contemporary dance video I'd posted. When it ended, Tilly and I, seated side by side at the dining room table with our parents, waited for the verdict.

"Well, I think the site is beautiful, Tatum. Very professional. I believe that new tablet will be a wise investment." My dad was not a naive man. He knew better than to comment on Tilly's dancing.

I beamed. The money I'd earned over the course of the summer was almost double what I needed to pay the commonwealth attorney, so I'd be picking up my gorgeous new device very soon.

"Tatum was amazing," Tilly offered. "I think TLC is going to be a huge success."

I beamed at her. "It's easy when you have good material to work with." Tilly beamed back.

Blanche was braver than my dad. "I agree. I should hire you to do something for me, Tatum. And I actually prefer this contemporary to your ballet, Matilda. So expressive. We could use more of that in our lives, I think."

No one spoke for the longest time; the only sound in the room was Belén inhaling and exhaling loudly and deliberately, tapping one red nail on the table. Some things never changed.

"This is what you want, Matilda?" Belén's voice was firm, but I could see she was trying to be reasonable. She definitely wasn't angry. Her lip wasn't quivering this time, but I thought I detected a tear. Hearing how not one daughter but two had defied her under her nose had to be rough. I felt a little bad for her, but was impressed she was taking it so well.

Tilly's face broke out into a tentative smile. "Yes, Mama. I love it."

Belén nodded. "Well. Then we will have to do some additional college research." She rose from the table, ending our family meeting, but then turned back to me. "I also think the website looks professional, Tatum." To my surprise, she even smiled. I knew she meant it by the crinkles in the corners of her eyes.

And, of course, I smiled back.

Chapter 18

The doorbell rang and sent a jolt of anticipatory electricity down my chest. I stood in front of the full-length mirror one last time, making sure my hair was behaving and that I didn't have mascara clumps on my cheeks. As I completed my final inspection, I heard the front door open, and my dad called up the stairs.

"Tatum? You have company."

I smoothed the fabric of my skirt, slid on my silver sandals, and carried myself down to the door. I didn't want to appear too eager, but everything inside me wanted to bolt down the stairs and launch myself at the person introducing himself to my parents.

As expected, I walked in the living room just as my dad was extending his hand.

"Pleased to meet you, Mr. Elsea. I'm Seamus Kipsang." My dad and my date shook hands, and my dad, clearly pleased with the strength of my cellist's handshake, smiled.

"That's a good Irish name, son."

"Yes sir, my mother is from County Kerry." He turned to me and grinned, his sea-green eyes glittering. "Hi, Tate. You look beautiful."

"Thank you," I said, lashes down.

Belén stood off to the side, arms crossed—she was still Belén, after all—but with a welcoming smile on her face. Seamus raised a hand in greeting to her and she nodded politely, her smile widening.

"Well, we should probably get going," I said, wanting to go before the magic spell of congeniality currently over my house broke.

"What time should I have her back, sir?" Bonus points for asking about curfew. I wondered what time my dad would say.

"You have your phone, Tatum?" Dad asked. I nodded. "Good, just don't come in at the crack of dawn. We trust you." I did my best to resist asking if he was joking, because by the easy smile on his face, I could tell he meant it. And he'd said "we." Hearing that he and Belén trusted me felt a little bit like a fairy tale.

"Thanks, Dad." I kissed him on the cheek.

"Have a good time," Belén said as we walked to the door. I turned and looked her in the eye.

"Thank you, Belén. We will." There was no snark, no sarcasm. I meant it, and so did she. With Seamus lightly guiding me to the door, the tiny flutters that felt like hope and maybe happiness beat a cadence in my belly. Just as we were leaving, I caught a glimpse of Blanche, peeking around the doorway to the basement. She gifted me a knowing smile, and I gave her a tiny wave back.

As the door firmly shut behind us, Seamus threaded his fingers through mine, and we walked hand in hand to his car. He led me to the passenger's side and opened the door for me, like a perfect gentleman. I stopped myself from glancing back toward the house to see if my dad or Belén were peeking out from behind the curtains. I kind of hoped they were, though. They would see that Seamus was most definitely a good decision on my part. Fully parent-approved. He closed my door lightly once I was inside the car and came around to the driver's side.

"So where are you taking me?" I asked. I was dying to know what he had planned, but I was even more excited just to spend time with him. In person.

Seamus started the engine and backed us out of the driveway, just as cautiously as Tilly might. Another point in the parent-approval column. "Well, as it happens, the revival theater downtown is showing *Carrie*. It was kind of like the night planned itself when I saw that."

My eyes widened, and a smile broke out on my face. "That's almost spooky." For the millionth time this summer, I couldn't help wondering if Blanche wove some kind of magic spell over me to make this happen.

"Spooky, but awesome," Seamus said, grinning, as we left my neighborhood and started our drive into the city. "But before that, we're going to the greatest burger place known to man, if you're up for it." My stomach rumbled in agreement, and he laughed. "I'll take that as a yes. And do you want to know the best part?" His voice was gleeful, like he couldn't wait to share a secret with me.

"Yes, please tell me the best part." I couldn't keep the smile on my face from stretching to my ears.

"Three words. Toasted. Marshmallow. Milkshakes."

"Sold. Drive faster."

When Seamus stopped at the last red light before the onramp to the highway that would take us to what was sounding like the most perfectly planned date in human history, his hand snaked around my waist and pulled me to him. He looked into my eyes with the same degree of longing that had captured my attention while he played. The flutters increased and, even while seated, my knees went weak. In one fluid motion, Seamus' lips found mine, lush and sweet, and I kissed him back, intoxicated. Even all my imaginings weren't as good as the real thing. When he pulled away, he kissed my forehead and exhaled.

"I needed a hello kiss."

I giggled into the crook of his neck. "Does that mean no good night kiss?"

"Of course not. If you play your cards right, you might get a middle-of-the-date-just-because kiss too."

"I hope so. I'll do my best."

"Of course you will. How could you not?" He winked, and the light turned green, sending us on our way once more.

When he parked the car in front of the restaurant, I grabbed his hand before he could get out.

"Hold on a sec, I almost forgot something." I reached into my purse, my fingers grazing the silver keychain, back in its rightful place, and pulled out the envelope I'd shoved in there that morning. Seamus looked at me, puzzled, but opened it and pulled out the card I'd painstakingly written that morning.

> Dear Seamus,
>> I realized I never thanked you for my song. So thank you. For that, and for everything.
>> Cheers to us.
>
>> Yours,
>> Tate

"My stepmother is a stickler about manners," I told him.

Seamus smiled and blushed. "You're welcome." He leaned over and pressed a kiss into my cheek. "Ready to go?"

I smiled and winked back. "I've always been ready."

"I believe that." He chuckled and hopped out.

Waiting for him to come around to my side, I sat still in the car for a moment, just letting the moment soak in. Everything I had been afraid of back in June was gone. My fears had been replaced with truths—about my family, my friends, myself—better than I could have hoped for. I felt as light as a feather.

My door opened, bringing me out of my head.

"Are you still with me, Tate?" Seamus asked, amused.

I blinked at him, disbelieving that he was standing over me, waiting just for me, the object of so many of my daydreams turned reality. He was the exclamation point at the end of a particularly long and frustrating, yet ultimately satisfying, chapter in the book of my life.

"Yeah. I'm good. Really good. Today kind of feels like the answer to a wish I made at the beginning of the summer."

"And did it come true?" The corners of his mouth tipped up in a slow smile.

Nothing this summer had gone the way I imagined. But maybe it was supposed to be that way so I could turn the page and move onto a new, fresh chapter in my story.

I smiled back. "Yes. It came true."

Q&A with Author Christina June

1. What made you decide to write a Cinderella retelling?

   I actually have a good story for this. I work in a school, and the Monday morning after the homecoming dance, I was walking into my building and spied an abandoned girls' dress shoe—a sparkly, strappy sandal—laying on the side of the road. It felt like a sign that I needed to write a Cinderella story. But I knew I wanted my heroine to question the rules she was given and push back against them. Et voilà, Tatum was born.

2. If you were a fairy tale character, who would you want to be?

   I have a young daughter, so most of my fairy tales come via Disney these days. Though I'd like a little more of Mulan's bravery and Tiana's drive and innovation, most days I'm an Anna—she's awkward, but she's got a great sense of humor—and I'm okay with that.

3. What elements of the Cinderella were the most fun to work into the story?

   The glass slipper/keychain took a little while to figure out, but once I did, I fell in love with it. A lot of the smaller elements that got layered in during revisions were really fun too. For example, Tilly makes a reference to cutting off part of her foot. That makes me laugh every time I read it.

4. Which character is the most like their Cinderella
counterpart?

*Probably Blanche, our fairy godmother. Anyone who likes the
Golden Girls and romance novels, is virtually psychic, and
wins at bunco on the first shot has to be magical, right?*

5. Tatum is certainly not the type of girl who sits around
and waits for her happy ending—she creates her own.
What do you love most about Tatum?

*Tatum is me. Tatum is, in many ways, every girl. I love that
she thinks she's right so fiercely, but figures out that her father
and stepmother actually might have had a valid reason for
asking her to think about her actions for a while. Too harsh a
punishment? For sure. They totally went overboard. But the
reflection time was good for her, and even Tatum would agree
with that.*

6. Friendship plays a huge role in this story. What do
you think Tatum learns from her new friends and her
friendship breakups?

*I think Tatum learns hope from Seamus, Abby, and Hunter.
They accept her just as she is, and encourage her to pursue
her art. From Ashlyn, she learns how to forgive. Even though
they're angry at each other, Tatum puts herself in Ash's shoes
and finds it within herself take the high road. I think they both
come out on the other side stronger and more empathic.*

7. Do you have any artistic talents like Tatum, or are you living vicariously through her?

   Besides writing? Once upon a time, I sang second soprano in the school choir and was a card-carrying member of the thespian society. In tenth grade, I was in Oklahoma! and said, "Who's going to be the auctioneer?" It was a big moment.

8. Even though Blanche doesn't have *real* magic, she's the perfect fairy godmother. What's the most important thing Blanche teaches Tatum?

   I love Blanche. She's one of my top five favorite characters I've written. She reminds Tatum that things are not always as they seem, and that sometimes you just need to look harder to see the truth. Blanche also reminds Tatum to do self-care and be good to herself. It's easy to forget that part when you're stressed or caught up in something.

9. If you could have dinner with one of your characters, who would it be?

   I think I'd like to have dessert with Blanche, Tatum, Tilly, and Abby, while The Frisson serenaded us.

10. Tatum and SK fall for each other through words and music. What's your favorite (love) song?

    Even before I wrote this book, I thought Sarah Jarosz's "Tell Me True" was incredibly romantic. She captures the emotions when you know you have feelings for someone and you suspect they feel the same, but you're waiting for the magical thing that confirms it. It's the moment before the fall. It was the perfect song for Tatum and Seamus.

My favorite love song, though, is Ben Folds' "The Luckiest," which my husband and I danced to at our wedding. I appreciate that Folds talks about how all your life experiences, no matter how rough, can be worth it because they brought you to the right person. And, if you're lucky, you get to spend your whole life together. Obviously, Folds is another favorite of mine, as his music appears in the book as well.

Acknowledgments

There will never be the right words to express my gratitude to everyone who left a piece of themselves in this book. There are virtual hugs included in these pages.

Thank you from the bottom of my heart:

To Kevan Lyon, my very wise agent, for finding Tatum's story captivating and delightful, and for always being the voice of reason. To Patricia Nelson, for all your support and positive energy.

To my editor, Jillian Manning, for falling in L-O-V-E with this book and being my champion since day one. To the entire team at Blink. I couldn't have asked for a more supportive, attentive, hard-working group of individuals to have on my side.

To Melissa Donoghue, my oldest and dearest friend in the world. There's no one I'd rather talk books with. Here's to another thirty years of friendship, and then thirty more.

To Amy Burns, my first writing friend, for loving all my words, even the terrible ones.

To the BAMFs, I love you all. This book would be nothing without you—Katherine Locke, Leigh Smith, Rebekah Campbell, Rebecca Paula, and Sarah Emery. MTWBWY, and I wish you all the dresses with pockets.

To Amanda Summers for putting up with, and also participating in, my nonsense. To Suzette Henry for your unwavering patience and enthusiasm—may our marble tables remain unbroken. To Esher Hogan, Jennifer Street, Diane Springer, and Alex Pou for your invaluable insight.

To Olivia Hinebaugh, Lisa Maxwell, Heather Van Fleet, Angele McQuaid, and Danielle Ellison for your friendship, understanding, and general awesomeness.

To Corey Ann Haydu for writing the book that made me want to make this one better.

To everyone in YADC. I am in awe of your unbridled love for words. There are no greater book pushers.

To my fellow 2017 debuts. It is an honor to be in your company, and I am thrilled to share this year with you.

To the entire YA writing and reading community. You inspire me to do more, and to do it better.

To my Pennsylvania and Florida family for always cheering me on. To Grandma for lending me your name.

To my parents for saving every last poem and short story, for never saying no when I handed you a stack of books to buy, and for knowing I'd write my own book one day, even when I didn't.

To my husband and my daughter, my buddies. I love you more than anything. Thank you for holding my hand and dreaming the big dreams with me.

And, to the girl who lost her shoe on the side of the road after the Homecoming dance. There would be no book without you.

Christina June writes young adult contemporary fiction when she's not writing college recommendation letters during her day job as a school counselor. She loves the little moments in life that help someone discover who they're meant to become—whether it's her students or her characters. Christina is a voracious reader, loves to travel, eats too many cupcakes, and hopes to one day be bicoastal—the east coast of the US and the east coast of Scotland. She lives just outside Washington, D.C., with her husband and daughter. Learn more at ChristinaJune.com.

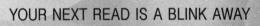